VALLEY of LOST SECRETS

The Valley of Lost Secrets

LESLEY PARR

BLOOMSBURY
CHILDREN'S BOOKS
LONDON OXFORD NEW YORK NEW DELHI SYDNEY

BLOOMSBURY CHILDREN'S BOOKS
Bloomsbury Publishing Plc
50 Bedford Square, London WC1B 3DP, UK

BLOOMSBURY, BLOOMSBURY CHILDREN'S BOOKS and the Diana logo
are trademarks of Bloomsbury Publishing Plc

First published in Great Britain in 2021 by Bloomsbury Publishing Plc

A catalogue record for this book is available from the British Library

ISBN: PB: 978-1-5266-2052-1; eBook: 978-1-5266-2050-7

2 4 6 8 10 9 7 5 3 1

Typeset by RefineCatch Limited, Bungay, Suffolk

Printed and bound in Great Britain by CPI Group (UK) Ltd, Croydon CR0 4YY

FSC www.fsc.org
MIX
Paper from
responsible sources
FSC® C020471

For Mammy

CHAPTER ONE

A DIFFERENT TYPE OF COUNTRYSIDE

There isn't as much sky as I thought there'd be. And what I can see is clear and blue, not the never-ending rain clouds we were told we'd get in Wales.

The guard blows his whistle and the train hoots back. I watch it pull away and my heart squeezes a bit. I want to get back on. I don't know why; it's not as if it's going back to London.

We've been through three stations today – from Paddington to Cardiff Central to here. This one's tiny, with only one platform. It's like our lives are shrinking. I straighten Ronnie's tag and we join the back of the line.

Dad said we'd be able to see for miles and miles in the countryside. He got us some library books with pictures of fields and hedgerows with little houses dotted around. But this isn't like that.

Massive, looming bulges of land – mountains, I suppose – have stolen most of the sky. I turn on the spot. They're all around, as though the village was dropped into the middle of a big fat cushion. Before now, the closest thing to a mountain I'd ever seen was a sand dune on Camber Sands. And it wasn't green. And it didn't have houses stuck on the side of it.

There's a tug at my sleeve. Ronnie's looking at me, eyes wide and teary. I lean down so he can whisper in my ear.

'This isn't like the pictures,' he says, sniffing.

'I know.'

'But Dad said—'

'He didn't know, did he? He didn't know we were coming here. He just knew it wasn't a city.' I look around again. 'There must be different types of countryside.'

'Well, this is the wrong type.' Ronnie sticks out his bottom lip.

This is all I need – a sulky little brother. No one will pick us if he looks a proper misery guts.

'Be quiet and try to look like a nice boy,' I say, making sure the string of his gas mask box sits properly on his shoulder. 'Nice and smart.'

I look over his head to the far end of the platform. The smoke's thinning, but it still stings my eyes and catches in my throat. I can see the face of the station clock now; it's almost teatime. The sign is clear too:

LLANBRYN

Funny word. Too many Ls.

Here we are, a wriggling, squiggling line of schoolchildren. Duff's at the front with his little sister. She's even younger than Ronnie; too young to understand any of this. I can't see many faces; most are looking at our teacher, Miss Goodhew. Some of us seem excited, some curious, but I bet everyone's nervous. Even the ones pretending not to be. Maybe even Duff.

Ronnie's crying again. It's OK for little brothers to cry but big brothers have to be the brave ones. Not that I would cry, anyway. I'm twelve. He watches sadly as a guard puts our suitcases in a pile near the gate at the end of the platform.

'I want my Dinky van,' he splutters.

'You can't have it. It's packed. You know what Nan said.'

'But—'

'Ronnie, it's safe,' I say. 'Remember how well you wrapped it in your pyjamas? You did a really good job there.'

He nods and blinks back more tears. I know he's trying to be brave too.

Next to the guard, Miss Goodhew is talking to a man and a woman. The man is tall and has a thick overcoat buttoned over his large stomach, and he's got the biggest moustache I've ever seen. The woman's all done up like she's in her Sunday best. She's walking down the line now, giving out custard creams as she counts us. When she gives one to Lillian Baker, Lillian thanks her for having us in their village. Duff's close enough to pull her plaits but he doesn't. He's not usually worried about getting into trouble; perhaps he *is* nervous. I bet Lillian Baker will get picked first. She's got long dark hair and her socks never fall down and all the grown-ups say she's pretty.

When the woman hands a biscuit to Ronnie, she stops and wipes away his tears with her hanky. She's got a metal badge pinned to her coat that says *WVS Housewives Service Identification*.

'What's your name?' she asks. Ronnie gulps and says nothing.

Now that she's close, I can smell lavender and peppermints. She lifts Ronnie's tag and says, 'Ronald, now that's one of my favourite names, that is.'

'We call him Ronnie,' I say, a bit harder than I mean to.

But she keeps on smiling, eyeing my tag. 'And you're a Travers too. Ronnie's brother, is it? So are you a James or a Jimmy?'

'Jimmy.'

'All right then,' she says. She gives me a custard cream and moves back up the line.

'She smells like Nan,' Ronnie whispers. His lip's wobbling again, so I take his hand and give it a squeeze, just like Dad would do.

'Eat your biscuit,' I say.

Miss Goodhew claps her hands and calls out to us. We all go quiet.

'These nice people are Mr and Mrs Bevan,' she shouts down the platform, using her fake-posh voice. 'They are here to take us up to the institute.'

I wonder what an institute is. It sounds grim.

'Welcome to Llanbryn!' Mr Bevan booms. I'm not surprised he booms. He looks like a boomer.

I glance at the sign again. It doesn't look like it says what *he* just said. Ronnie's copying him, screwing up his face, trying to make his mouth fit around the letters.

'Lll … clll … cllaaa …'

'Stop it,' I whisper. 'No one will pick us if they think you're simple.'

'Don't worry about your cases,' Mr Bevan says. 'We've got men taking them up for you.'

Ronnie tightens his grip on my hand and I know he's thinking about his Dinky van again. Those men – whoever they are – had better be careful with his case. If he loses that van, he won't stop crying till the end of the war.

We set off, our gas mask boxes bumping against us. Mrs Bevan and Miss Goodhew chat at the head of the line. Mr Bevan waits as we cross the road outside the station, then joins Ronnie and me at the back.

'Are you ready for your adventure, boys?' he asks, grinning.

What's he talking about? Adventures happen in jungles or on raging rivers or in the Wild West. Not here. Not in Wales with a whimpering little brother and a custard cream.

Ronnie's stopped crying, so that's something. He's twisted the top off his biscuit and is licking the creamy bit.

'Are we going up there?' he asks, his eyes darting nervously from Mr Bevan to the mountainside houses.

Mr Bevan nods. 'We are.'

'It's a long way up,' Ronnie says.

Mr Bevan turns to the houses and tilts his head from side to side. A big grin breaks out on his face, stretching his moustache and making him look like a happy walrus.

'Not for a big strong boy like you!'

Ronnie beams.

'Come on then!' Mr Bevan ruffles Ronnie's hair. I smooth it down again. No one will pick us if he looks a proper mess. I might not want to be here, but I don't fancy us being the last ones chosen, either – the dregs in the bottom of a bottle.

We start to climb a wide track. Bushes and trees grow on either side. Ronnie asks if it's a forest. I catch Mr Bevan's eye and see his moustache twitch over his smile.

'Stop asking stupid questions,' I hiss in Ronnie's ear.

Then, up ahead, Duff's little sister drops her custard cream. She stops dead and just stays there until her face turns a greyish shade of blue. I've seen her do this lots of times before, when we've been out playing, but Mr Bevan looks horrified.

'What's she doing?' he asks.

'Holding her breath,' I answer. 'She can only do it for so long, then she really starts.'

'Starts what?'

'Wait for it.'

I don't know if it's got anything to do with the mountains curving all round us, but her wails are even louder here, not far off an air-raid siren. The two women rush over to her and Mrs Bevan opens her handbag. She feels around inside, pulls out a chocolate bar and snaps off a piece.

'Dairy Milk,' Ronnie groans. 'I should've dropped *my* biscuit.'

As we move off, Florence Campbell picks up the custard cream and stuffs it in her pocket. I pretend not to see. I don't think Florence can believe her luck – two biscuits in one day. I bet she's never had two biscuits in her whole life.

We keep climbing until we reach another road. We follow it round the corner until an enormous brown-brick building comes into view. It's three storeys high, bulky and strong-looking.

'I'll just catch up with Miss Goodhew and my wife at the front,' Mr Bevan says. 'You two wait by here.'

'Jimmy calls her Miss Badhew,' Ronnie says, 'because she isn't nice, so she can't be a *good* hew, can she?'

'Ronnie!' I mutter.

But Mr Bevan is laughing. 'Don't worry, Jimmy. We had nicknames for teachers when I was a boy too.'

He walks away and I can't believe I haven't been told off.

'Here we are,' he says, standing in the arched doorway. He looks really proud, like he's showing us Buckingham Palace. 'The Llanbryn Miners Institute.'

I look from Mr Bevan to the institute. They match, the way some people do with their dogs. There's something about him that says he belongs here, like he's a part of this place. But that just makes me feel even more like an outsider.

'Everyone's in the main hall. They can't wait to see you.'

The room is massive, much bigger than our school hall. It's all dark timber, polished up till it shines.

There are steps and a raised platform at the far end, a bit like a stage. The room's bursting with people all staring and muttering; surely they can't all want an evacuee? Some must be here to gawp. They sit in rows in front of the platform and, as we walk past them to the raised bit, I can feel the place swallowing us up – my little brother, all the others and me.

CHAPTER TWO

SCARED CITY RABBITS

Mrs Bevan steers all of us evacuees on to the stage, helping the littlest ones up the small steps. Ronnie's sticky hand slips into mine.

'Jimmy,' he whispers, 'what if no one picks us?'

I look down at him, at his little cowlick fringe and big doe eyes. 'Don't be silly. Who wouldn't want us?' I don't tell him I'm terrified that no one will.

It's so noisy. People are talking, shifting in their seats, coughing. There are a lot more villagers than evacuees. That has to be a good thing, increase our chances. If there are more of them than of us, Ronnie and me can't be left behind. Some men bring in our cases and Mrs Bevan shows where to put them on the floor in front of us. Mr Bevan steps on to the stage and the hall goes quiet. Ronnie's gripping my hand so tight it's starting to hurt but I don't care. All that matters is that someone wants us.

Mr Bevan clears his throat and says in his booming voice, 'As president of the Miners Institute and representative of the people of Llanbryn, I'd like to welcome our London visitors.'

He turns and waves an arm towards us as if we're being revealed in a magic trick. Twenty-six scared city rabbits waiting to be pulled out of a hat.

'Now, we'll do our best to get this done as quickly as possible,' Mr Bevan says, unfolding a sheet of paper. 'Miss Goodhew and the children have had a very long and tiring journey.'

I watch his eyes travel down the page. Ronnie's trembling. I drag my hand out of his and put my arm around his shoulder, pulling him close to me. He takes a big, shuddering breath and lets it out into my side. I feel the warmth of it through my jacket.

'I have the Joneses …' Mr Bevan says. Quite a few people stand up and Mr Bevan laughs but I don't get why it's funny. He carries on, 'I mean Ralph and Megan … those Joneses.'

I wonder how many Joneses are in this place. All the people, except a young-looking couple on the front row, sit down again.

'Down for one girl, I see,' Mr Bevan says.

The woman nods and points at Lillian Baker, who almost does a curtsy before moving along the stage and down the steps.

Lillian Baker first. I knew it.

Someone shuffles behind me; I look around to see Florence Campbell trying to smooth down her hair. It won't make any difference; there are so many nits it's practically moving on its own. She sees me looking and pokes out her tongue. I edge forward so no nits can jump on me. Ronnie caught them once and Nan had to rub his head with Lethane oil; he wailed for hours and coughed for weeks. No wonder the nits cleared off.

Duff and his sister go next with a woman whose nose is so far in the air I'm surprised she can see where she's going. A woman in a huge purple hat says in a loud voice that they are lucky little children. Duff glances back and gives me the thumbs up. I try to smile but it gets stuck halfway and I'm sure I must look properly daft.

Ronnie's face is still buried in my jacket. I haven't seen him like this since Mum went.

'Come on,' I whisper, 'it's like Mr Bevan said, this is an adventure, yeah?'

He sniffs and peers around the hall. Mrs Bevan smiles at him and mouths, 'Chin up.' Ronnie sticks his chin into the air and I almost laugh.

The hall's emptying quite quickly now – some evacuees go happily, some cry. A tall man with a smiley face takes the four Turners together. He and his wife hold their hands as they leave, two children each. Mr Bevan called him Dr Jenkins so I suppose he must have a big house.

About half of us have gone when a round, flushed woman wearing a flowered apron hurries in. She rolls her eyes and shakes her head like she's laughing at herself.

'Sorry, sorry!' she says, coming to the front of the hall. 'Can I go next, please, Ceri? I've had to shut the shop, see.'

My heart beats faster; she's got a shop. Even if rationing starts, I reckon an evacuee would do all right with a shopkeeper. Especially if it's a *sweet* shop.

'Come on then, Phyllis,' says Mr Bevan, checking his list. 'No preference for a boy or a girl, as long as it's just the one. Is that correct?'

Just the one. Angry tears prick at my eyes.

The woman gives us all the quick once-over and her gaze settles somewhere behind Ronnie and me.

'That girl,' she says gently.

'The one scratching her head?' Mr Bevan asks.

Florence! Florence Campbell is being picked before us! Picked before some of the other girls,

girls with clean faces and cardies with all the buttons on!

Florence steps off the stage. As she passes, I hear her breath quick and hard. I get a whiff of her smell; like when our old dog used to come in from the rain and dry off by the fire. The woman puts her arm around Florence. I can't believe it – no one ever touches a Campbell – you get Campbell Germs that never wash off. That's what Duff says.

Phyllis the shop woman and Florence leave the hall too.

Mr Bevan calls the next name on the list. Mrs Thomas. A fair-haired woman gets up from one of the middle rows, her eyes on Ronnie. Some people whisper and make huffing noises. Mr Bevan glares at them and she nods to him as if to say thank you, then smiles at Ronnie. He giggles.

This is it; we won't be last.

'One boy, I believe,' Mr Bevan says.

One.

I think I might really be sick, properly sick, all over my shoes sick. I just want to go home.

I'm gripping Ronnie's shoulder so tight I must be hurting him but he's just watching her. Then the woman called Mrs Thomas looks at me and I get the same smile.

'I've changed my mind, Ceri,' she says. 'We can make room for two.'

CHAPTER THREE

21 HEOL MABON

We get off the stage and Mrs Thomas holds out her hand to Ronnie. He reaches for it but I pull him closer. She looks at me and nods her head once and I notice that her eyes are really, really blue.

'I'll just take the suitcases then, shall I?' she says. Her voice is soft and goes up and down.

I say nothing. A few people nudge each other. The woman in the purple hat frowns and shakes her head. Maybe they think Mrs Thomas can't make room for two?

'Follow me, boys,' she says. 'You can carry your gas masks.'

We follow. Outside, I look up at those mountains again – they make me feel smaller than Ronnie.

'Well, you already know I'm Mrs Thomas but you must call me Gwen. Aunty Gwen if you like.' She swaps the cases around in her hands. I don't offer to take one – and I'm not calling her 'Aunty' either. 'Turn right here, boys, up the hill.'

Another flipping hill.

'And what are your names then?' she asks.

'Ronnie,' Ronnie says. 'And my big brother is Jimmy.'

She smiles and looks right at me, like she's taking me in. I put my head down and keep walking, the backs of my knees tightening with every step. It's no bother for Mrs Thomas though; she's hardly out of breath, even with the cases. Rows of terraced houses lead off the hill on both sides. Each street looks the same and each house has a front step that meets the pavement.

'It isn't just me, mind, there's my husband as well,'

she says. 'Alun. But you won't see him today; he's over in Aberbeeg building a shelter for my cousin Jean. He's a collier so you'll have to be quiet when he's on nights. He sleeps in the day then. And if you can't manage that then you can go out to play. But don't go far. And always tell me where you'll be.'

Play where? All I can see are houses and fields stuck on the side of a mountain.

'What's a collier?' Ronnie asks.

'Oh, of course!' Even her laugh has a Welsh accent. 'You boys wouldn't know, would you? A collier is another name for a miner. Most of the families round here are mining families.'

After three more streets with names I can't pronounce, we turn right again. The sign says Heol Mabon; I think I might be able to manage that. Almost every door is open as women, old people and children watch us move along the pavement. Some are smiling, but others, like the woman in the purple hat at the institute, frown. Mrs Thomas says hello to them all. Some try to talk to her but she says she has to get us home; we've had a long journey.

'Home' isn't the word I'd use.

We stop outside a dark blue front door. 'This is us,' Mrs Thomas says. 'Number twenty-one.' Someone opens an upstairs window of the house next door. A tiny, thousand-year-old woman with grey hair up in a bun waves a duster at us. Her eyes and nose are really small but her mouth is wide in her wrinkly face. She looks like a tortoise.

'Got two, have you, Gwen?' she calls. 'Thought you were only going for one. How will you manage?'

I already feel like a parcel, wrapped up, labelled and sent far away. The tortoise is making it worse. Mrs Thomas whispers to us, 'Take no notice of Mrs Maddock, we've got room.'

To the old woman she says, in a much tighter voice, 'We'll manage fine, Menna.'

I'm sure Mrs Thomas adds '*nosy old bat*' under her breath as she goes inside, which makes me want to like her but I don't know if I should. Ronnie follows but I hang back. The passage is dark but not gloomy; there's a closed door to the right – probably the parlour – and stairs ahead. Mrs Thomas and Ronnie go through another door further down.

I walk after them, through a living room into the kitchen that smells of Lux soap. It's got a stove at one end with washing hanging over it, just like Nan's washday back home. I swallow down the lump in my throat. From the window above the sink, I can see a small yard that looks like it leads round to the back garden. Mrs Thomas points to a table and chairs and tells us to sit down. Without even asking if we're hungry, she starts cutting bread, then gives us each a slice with margarine on. 'That'll do you till tea. I'm going to take your things upstairs; you stay here and eat up. Oh! Before I do ...' She opens a drawer, pulls out a pair of scissors and snips off our name tags. 'Now that's better. Shows you belong here, see.'

I don't know where we belong any more but it's not here.

'Have you got any boys or girls?' Ronnie asks, watching Mrs Thomas over the top of his slice. 'Or are they big now?'

She pauses and her smile doesn't look completely real.

'Don't you ever listen?' I say. 'She said it was just her and Mr Thomas, cloth ears!'

'It's all right, Jimmy.' She turns to him. 'No we don't, Ronnie – but it means we have room for you. That's nice, isn't it?'

She leaves. Ronnie watches her go.

'I like Aunty Gwen,' he says. 'When she talks it sounds like she's singing.' He smiles and licks some margarine off his bread.

'Stop licking your food,' I say. 'You're not a blooming kitten – and don't call her Aunty.'

'Can if I like, she said so.'

'Well, I'm saying not to. I'm your family, not her.'

He looks right at me, his big green eyes searching mine. Just like she did. Then he miaows and licks his bread again and I laugh.

After ten minutes, Mrs Thomas calls us up to the bedroom. It's small and narrow with a window to the left. She's standing in front of a chest of drawers. Our empty cases lie open on top of a candlewick bedspread.

One bed.

'Your things are here,' she says, opening and closing the drawers one at a time to show us.

'I could've done that,' I say quickly.

'You could have carried your case too, but you didn't.'

It feels like she's scolding me but I'm not sure because she's smiling. Ronnie steps closer to the bed and looks in the cases, then his eyes dart around the room. He goes over to the drawers and pulls them open. I can see the panic building in him and I know what he's looking for. The trouble is, I can't see it either.

'What is it? What's the matter?' Mrs Thomas is staring at him.

'He's looking for his Dinky van,' I say. 'It's yellow.'

'Oh my goodness, it's here!' She pulls the little metal toy out of her skirt pocket. 'I'm so sorry, Ronnie. It fell out of your pyjamas and I picked it up and slipped it in here.'

He takes it off her and clutches it tight to him.

'He loves it,' I explain. 'And he had to pack it with his clothes in case he lost it on the journey.'

'Nan made me,' he mutters grumpily.

'He isn't usually allowed to take it out of the house any more,' I say. 'Not since he lost it in the sand on holiday, but Nan said he could bring it here because he can't sleep without it.'

Other little boys sleep with teddies or bunnies, but not my brother.

'She said we might be here for lots of weeks,' Ronnie says.

'But we won't,' I say.

Mrs Thomas looks at me like she's a bit sorry for me, like I don't know anything about the war because I'm twelve. But she smiles at Ronnie. 'Then we'll take extra-special care of it here, won't we?'

He nods.

She points at the single bed. 'It'll be a bit of a squeeze. There's just this at the moment but you can bunk up, can't you? The bedspread's lovely and soft and we'll get another mattress as soon as we can.'

'We don't mind, do we, Jimmy?' Ronnie says, sitting on the bed. 'As long as we're together. That was my brother's worst worry, that we'd be split up.'

I don't know why he had to tell her that. It's none of her business.

Mrs Thomas puts the cases on top of the wardrobe. 'You boys get settled, then come down when you're ready.' She closes the door behind her.

'I wonder what she sounds like when she really sings,' Ronnie says. 'Lillian Baker said Wales people sing all the time.'

'Welsh people.'

'What?'

'They're *Welsh*, not Wales. Wales is the country.'

'Oh.'

From the window, I can see the back garden. It's long, bigger than ours, and slopes up to a hedge that meets another garden. It looks a bit like the allotment Grandad used to have with its rows of vegetables and sticks that make a wigwam for runner beans. But Grandad's allotment was flat. Nothing in Llanbryn is flat. Next to their air-raid shelter is a pen with a little wooden hut in it. Up above the rows of rooftops are the mountains. They overlap each other, making it impossible to see what's behind them. I suppose it's more mountains. Like there's no way out.

So this is it. The countryside. Evacuation. No more getting covered in oil in the garage with Dad. No more Nan telling us off for it. Just other people's biscuits and houses and a single bed. None of it's ours.

I turn to Ronnie. He's running his fingers over the candlewick bedspread, tracing patterns in and out of the flowers and leaves. I know he's itching to tug out the fluffy bits; Nan's always telling him off for it.

I look around properly. We share at home but our bedroom's much bigger, big enough to play a really good game of cowboys. Dad let us have it after Mum left – said he preferred to be cosy – but I think he just didn't like it in there without her.

Ronnie pulls at the bedspread.

'No!' I yell.

He jumps and I feel bad. I sit next to him and put my arm around his shoulders.

'I'm sorry for shouting,' I say, 'but you can't do that, especially not here. Remember what Nan said?'

'To behave like we do at home.'

'Better. She said we have to behave *better* so we don't show her up. You don't want to show her up, do you?'

He shakes his head.

I fluff up the candlewick so the gaps don't show. Mrs Thomas was right; it is soft. 'This isn't our home, Ronnie, this isn't your bed.'

This isn't our home. Saying it out loud makes it even worse. I dig my fist into the pillow. Ronnie kneels up on the bed, both of his arms stretched around me.

'We'll be all right, Jimmy,' he says. 'You can have the bed if you like. I'll sleep on the floor. I don't mind.'

I have to smile. He thinks I'm upset about the bed. He doesn't get it. He never really gets it; Mum leaving, evacuation, the war. It must be nice to be six and daft.

CHAPTER FOUR

A BRICK OUTHOUSE

Tea is tomato soup, but not the Heinz one from a can we have at home. This is proper soup. Mrs Thomas made it from the tomatoes in the garden. She made the bread too. She asks us loads of questions and Ronnie chatters away about all sorts of nonsense. She tells us about living in Llanbryn but I don't listen much. I just dip my bread in my soup and wonder if bombs are falling on our house. When we've finished, Ronnie shows me up by sticking his face in the bowl, trying to lick it. Mrs Thomas tells him to mind his manners and he doesn't miaow this time.

She says we don't have to wash and dry on our first night so she gives us a board game. But snakes and ladders with Ronnie isn't much fun because he keeps landing on the wrong squares – although most of them are ladders, so I start to wonder if he's faking it.

There's a loud knock on the front door.

'Oh!' Mrs Thomas says from the kitchen. 'Who can that be?' She takes off her pinny and tosses it on the back of a chair on her way through the living room.

A voice booms down the passage.

'Mr Bevan!' Ronnie jumps up and follows her, looking thrilled to bits. I get up and watch from the living-room doorway.

'Well, look here,' Mr Bevan says, grinning at Ronnie. 'It's our little adventurer, isn't it?'

Ronnie nods, beaming up at him.

'And how do you like it in the Valleys?'

'It's nice. We had soup.'

'What kind?'

'Not from a can.'

'Ahh, that's the best flavour for soup, that is.' Mr Bevan turns to Mrs Thomas. 'How are you, Gwen? Margaret said Alun was away for the night …'

'Yes,' she says, 'he's doing a shelter for Jean and Ted. No buses back now till the morning. What can we do for you?'

Another voice comes from outside. 'Err … hello! Can you hurry up in there, like? My arms are dropping off – we aren't all built like a brick outhouse!'

'Righto, Dai.' Mr Bevan steps out for a second, then backs into the passage with one end of a mattress. 'Margaret sent us with this. It's from our spare room, she thought you'd need one with you taking both boys.'

'Oh my goodness!' Mrs Thomas gasps. 'That's so kind.'

'Back bedroom, Gwen?' Mr Bevan says, looking like he could carry the mattress under one arm.

She nods and they go up. Ronnie follows, telling them all that this will be his mattress.

I go into the living room and pack up the game.

*

I shine my torch on the alarm clock, then flick it off again. Ten past one and I haven't slept a wink. Ronnie fell asleep straight away, holding his Dinky van. I don't know how he can do it, in a new and strange place. A new and strange country. I bash my pillow a few times and try to get comfortable. Ronnie mumbles and turns over. It's too dark to see him but I know he looks like an angel. That's what Dad always says.

I've just shut my eyes when Ronnie starts to moan and whimper. I throw back the bedspread and sit up. He grunts, opens his eyes and starts shouting. I slip down on to the mattress and hold him tight until his breaths are normal again. His hot tears wet my pyjama sleeve.

There's a tapping sound. 'Are you boys all right in there?' Light makes a line under the door. It's Mrs Thomas.

'We're fine,' I whisper-shout. The door handle turns and I call out, 'Don't come in!'

She does anyway.

Worry shows on her face in the light from the landing. She steps towards us. 'Oh, Ronnie, bach.'

'He's all right,' I say, squeezing him tighter into me.

Her hand twitches as if she wants to comfort him.

'Honestly, Mrs Thomas, I'm used to this,' I say. 'We'll be fine by ourselves.'

Her voice comes out small and unsure. 'Well ... all right.' She watches us for a few seconds, then says, 'Tomorrow I'll show you where the park is. You'll like the swings, Ronnie, and Jimmy can push you. That'll be nice, won't it?'

He pulls away from me and nods.

'Night then,' she says. 'Don't be afraid to knock if you need me.'

'We won't need you.'

She raises her eyebrows.

'But thanks,' I say quickly.

Mrs Thomas goes out, closes the door and pads away along the landing. I have to sneaky-read Ronnie a whole story before he drops off again. I know how to look after him.

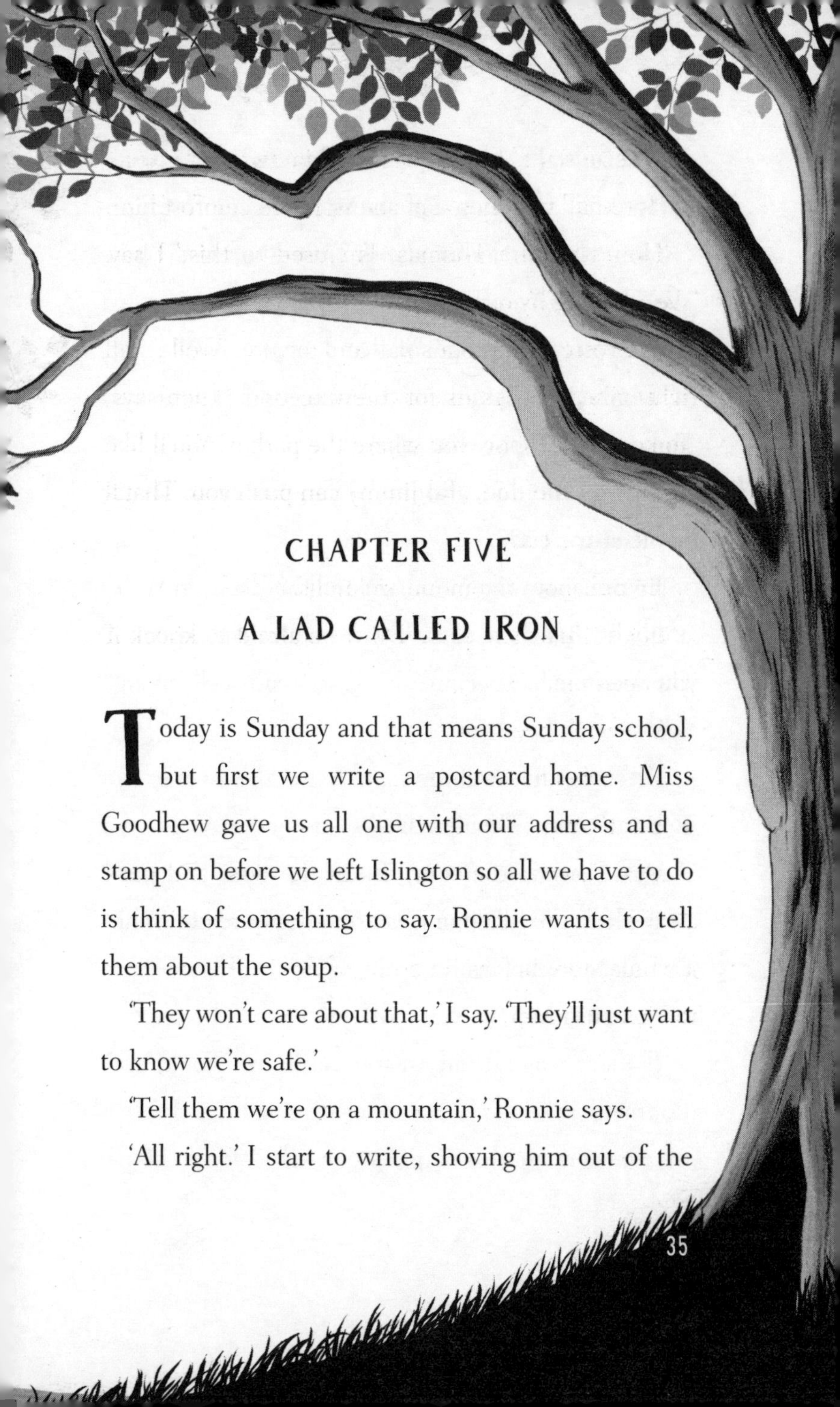

CHAPTER FIVE

A LAD CALLED IRON

Today is Sunday and that means Sunday school, but first we write a postcard home. Miss Goodhew gave us all one with our address and a stamp on before we left Islington so all we have to do is think of something to say. Ronnie wants to tell them about the soup.

'They won't care about that,' I say. 'They'll just want to know we're safe.'

'Tell them we're on a mountain,' Ronnie says.

'All right.' I start to write, shoving him out of the

way because he's pressing so close I can hardly see.

'Say that I slept on a mattress on the floor.'

Mrs Thomas looks across from the sink where she's peeling carrots. 'Oh no, they'll think we aren't looking after you properly!'

'Don't put that, then,' Ronnie says. 'I feel very looked after. Write that instead.'

'Just let me do it, Ronnie! Then you can put your name at the end.'

I write about the mountain and that we're in Wales and we miss them. I also write about the mattress. He won't know because he can't read well enough yet.

After breakfast and a push on the swings for Ronnie, Mrs Thomas walks us down 'the Bryn' towards the train station. She says that's the name of the hill we walked up yesterday. It already feels like a thousand years ago.

A thousand years since we saw Dad and Nan.

If there was a train on the platform I could grab Ronnie and jump on it and go back home and forget we ever came to this stupid green valley. Even though

I know we could never really do it, I'm still looking for the steam.

But we don't get as far as the station. Instead we stop across the road from the institute, on the pavement in front of a huge square building with a pointed roof but no steeple. The words *Tabernacle 1873* are carved into the stone above its tall arched windows. It's shaped more like a house than a chapel, and the windows and doors look almost like a face – not a smiley one but not a bad one either.

Mrs Thomas squats down next to Ronnie and points through the railings at a smaller, plainer building on the left. 'That's the Sunday School Hall.' She straightens his collar. 'The teacher is Miss Williams, she'll look after you. I'll come back in an hour when you're more holy.'

She winks at me. I look away.

'Aren't you coming in, Aunty Gwen?' Ronnie asks. I shoot him a *Don't call her that* look but his eyes are on her.

'No, I'm going home to get our dinner ready,' she says. 'Alun will be back soon.'

'Are you holy enough then?' Ronnie says, playing with the button on her coat.

I nudge him but Mrs Thomas laughs and says, 'Oh, don't you worry about me, I'll come back for the evening service. You go in now, Miss Williams is waiting.' And off she goes, back up the hill.

We walk along the pavement and up the path with two others. One's a lad of about fourteen, with dark hair sticking out from under his cap. He smiles at me but I don't feel like smiling back. The other is a fair girl with wavy hair who looks more my age. She pats her blue ribbon and doesn't look at me. She's probably stuck-up.

Halfway along the path, Ronnie pulls his hand from mine to wave and shout up the road. 'Goodbye, *Aunty* Gwen!' Then he runs into the hall.

The lad raises his eyebrows. 'That your little brother?'

'Yes,' I say, 'and he'll cop it later.'

The hall is plain, with benches in rows like pews, an aisle down the middle and a big cross at the front. Ronnie's just inside the door looking half pleased with himself and half jumpy – the way he always does when he's done something he shouldn't. I grab his sleeve and pull him over to a bench at the back.

On the one in front, two girls talk really fast in Welsh. It's like they want us to know just how far from home we are. I look around and see some other evacuees; the oldest Turner has the youngest on her lap. I wave and they wave back but there's no sign of Duff.

Miss Williams tells us they usually sing Welsh hymns but today they're singing them in English because of us. I think we're supposed to be grateful. Lillian Baker says that makes her feel really welcome in Llanbryn. Miss Williams says that Lillian must be very clever because she can say 'Llanbryn' so well.

One hundred and fifty miles from our school and Lillian Baker is still teacher's flaming pet!

We sing 'Jesus Loves Me'. At our Sunday school, Duff swaps the words for rude ones and we laugh behind our hymn books. But this time, when the hymn is over, there's nothing. I wish he was here; then maybe, just for a minute, it'd feel like evacuation never happened.

Miss Williams asks the dark-haired lad to read a Bible story. She says she's making the most of him because very soon he'll be a collier at the pit and working men go to chapel, not Sunday school.

I don't quite catch his name, it sounds something like 'Iron' but it can't be that. Even in Wales it can't be that. Before he goes to the front, he passes his cap to the girl with fair hair and she holds it tight to her chest like she's protecting it from the whole world. She reminds me of someone, but I can't think who it is.

At the end we say the Lord's Prayer. Miss Williams says we're going to learn it in Welsh next week. Lillian Baker looks so excited I think she might wet herself.

Ronnie and me go outside to wait for Mrs Thomas by the railings. A loud wail comes from across the road and there's Duff, trying to calm his little sister. He's with the woman who picked them at the institute. And there's someone else, another boy, skinny and shorter than Duff with straw-coloured hair. I call out and Duff waves but he doesn't come over. The boy gives me a dark look so I stare at him hard. They keep walking down the hill.

I turn to Ronnie but he isn't next to me like he's supposed to be. He's over by the chapel doorway with the fair girl and the lad who might be called Iron. Ronnie's got the lad's cap on; it's too big and slips down over his eyes, which makes him giggle.

The three of them start a game of blind man's buff, even though the lad's a bit old for it. The girl runs around and around Ronnie, tapping him on the shoulder. He spins and stumbles but doesn't fall because the lad catches him and sets him straight. The game starts again and Ronnie grabs the girl's arm. He pulls off the cap and they all laugh and laugh.

Anyone would think he was *their* brother.

The lad sees me watching. 'Want to play?' he says. 'You can be "it" if you like.'

I want to. But my feet won't move.

'Come on, Jimmy.' The girl comes closer, staring right at me like her words are a dare. 'Or don't you want to get *Campbell Germs*?'

Something crashes into my brain like a steam engine. There's no grimy face and no wet dog smell, but this is Florence Campbell. With clean clothes and a ribbon in her hair like a proper girl.

The lad and Ronnie come over too. Just then, Mrs Thomas rushes up the pavement. 'Not late, am I?'

'No, Gwen,' the lad says, 'Miss Williams finished a bit early today.'

'You'd better get back to the shop, I'm sure your mam will be needing some help with the papers.'

He puts his cap back on and grins at me. 'I'm Yiyun,' he says.

'It's spelled I-E-U-A-N,' says Florence. Her eyes are shining in a way I've never seen before. Her voice is challenging me to a fight.

Ieuan smiles at her. I think he likes her – but that doesn't make sense because no one likes Florence Campbell. It's a rule where we come from. But this isn't where we come from, everything and everyone is different. Even Florence is different.

But I feel just the same.

CHAPTER SIX

MR THOMAS

Roast beef!

The smell pulls us along the passage and into the living room like we're the Bisto Kids.

Mrs Thomas calls out, 'Hello, love, we're back. Now, boys, give me your coats and I'll hang them up. Go on, into the living room. Say hello.'

Mr Thomas is reading a newspaper in the biggest armchair next to the fireplace.

He looks over the top of it and nods his head.

'These are our special guests,' she says. 'Jimmy and Ronnie.'

'Boys,' he says.

That's all. He lifts the paper and disappears back behind a headline about tea rationing.

Mrs Thomas points to a low table in front of the fire; it's covered in comics. 'They're Ieuan's old ones. Phyllis sent them round with the paper boy. You have a look at them while I finish getting dinner ready. I've got a nice bit of beef to celebrate you being here.'

Celebrate? She must be as daft as Ronnie.

'Thanks, Aunty Gwen!' Ronnie says, picking his Dinky van off the table and putting it in his pocket. He dives on the pile of comics. It's all *Dandy*s and *Beano*s – loads of them. I try not to show I'm excited too.

'Read me this one, Jimmy!' Ronnie demands, pulling me down on to the settee next to him and holding up a *Beano*. I look over at Mr Thomas, still behind his paper. I can just see the top of his head, his dark hair slicked back with Brylcreem. Just like Dad's. His shirtsleeves are rolled up, showing big, hairy arms. His hands are clean but there's black stuff under his nails.

Halfway through *Lord Snooty*, I can tell Ronnie's stopped listening. He's watching Mr Thomas. Or, at least, watching the newspaper Mr Thomas is behind.

'Why won't he talk to us?' Ronnie whispers.

'I don't know, do I? Perhaps he doesn't want us here. They were only supposed to have one evacuee, remember.'

Oh heck, Ronnie's face is crumpling up. Why did I go and say that? The last thing we need is for Mr Thomas to think he's lumbered with a crybaby.

Mr Thomas lowers his paper, folds it and puts it on his lap. Leaning forward, he rests his elbows on top of it. Under his thick eyebrows, his eyes are like bits of coal. They're that black. But they shine like coal too, and I can tell he's not cross.

He looks from me to Ronnie. 'Two's fine.'

Again, that's all he says. Ronnie raises his eyebrows as if asking me a question.

'I don't flaming know, do I?' I say.

'Dinner's ready!' Mrs Thomas calls from the kitchen.

Ronnie looks confused. 'But we haven't had our lunch yet.'

Mr Thomas gets up from his chair. 'No one has lunch round here. Middle of the day is dinner.'

Ronnie looks like he's going to ask what they have at dinner-time but Mr Thomas has already gone into the kitchen.

We get up and follow him through. Mrs Thomas is standing by the stove, wiping her hands on her pinny. On the table are four plates with potatoes, carrots, cabbage, roast beef and the biggest Yorkshire puddings I've ever seen. They're like dinner bowls. Mr Thomas is sitting down, facing us.

'Come on then,' Mrs Thomas says, taking off her pinny and hanging it on a hook on the wall.

We sit. Ronnie takes his Dinky van out of his pocket, drives it around my fork and parks it next to his plate.

'Not on the table, please, Ronnie,' Mrs Thomas says.

Without looking up, he puts the van back in his pocket.

Mr Thomas picks up the gravy boat.

'Alun,' Mrs Thomas says. She says it gently but there's a warning in it too.

He sighs and puts it down again. 'Carry on.' He leans back, his hands behind his head.

She puts her hands together and closes her eyes. We do the same but I peep through my eyelashes. Mr Thomas just sits there, looking at the ceiling. I half expect him to whistle.

'For what we are about to receive, may the Lord make us truly thankful. Amen,' says Mrs Thomas.

'Amen,' says Ronnie.

'Amen,' I say.

Mr Thomas says nothing, just picks the gravy boat back up and gives it to Ronnie. I quickly put my hands over his – I have to help him pour or there'll be none left for anyone else.

Ronnie lifts a forkful of beef to his mouth.

'Not yet,' I mutter. 'Wait till everyone's got gravy.'

The fork hovers an inch from his lips, eyes following the gravy boat, until we've all taken our turn.

'Our nan never makes food like this,' Ronnie says, shovelling carrots into his mouth and dribbling gravy on his chin. Mrs Thomas gets up, takes a cloth from a drawer and wipes the gravy off. I want to say he can wipe his own chin but I don't.

'Gwen's the best cook in South Wales,' Mr Thomas says, like he really does know all the cooks in South Wales.

Mrs Thomas pretends to be embarrassed. I say nothing. This is probably the best meal I've ever had but I'm not going to let them know that.

'Boys,' she says, 'I have some news about school.'

Ronnie and me glance at each other.

'I was talking to Margaret Bevan this morning, she's the lady who brought you up from the station—'

'The one who smells like Nan?' Ronnie asks.

The Thomases look confused.

'Lavender and peppermints,' I mutter.

Mrs Thomas smiles and carries on, 'Anyway, she said there's been a problem with the pipes in St Michael's church hall. They were going to use it for your lessons, you see, there's no room at the school.'

'So what's happening instead?' I ask.

'Nothing. For now. It's going to be a few weeks until it's fixed so you're having an extra-long summer holiday.'

'Jimmy! No school!' Ronnie beams.

I don't beam. In Islington, this would have been great – cricket in the park with Duff, helping Dad at the garage – but what good are longer holidays in the middle of nowhere?

'The only other places would be the chapel hall or the institute,' Mrs Thomas carries on, 'but they're being used for the war effort. Although, if you ask me, children going to school should be a priority over Hilda Ringrose and Ruth Evans knitting socks for soldiers just to make themselves look good.' She stops suddenly, covering her mouth.

Mr Thomas pats her arm. 'Another few weeks won't turn the boys into dunces, Gwen.'

'What will Miss Badhew do?' asks Ronnie.

'Mrs Bevan has asked Miss *Good*hew,' Mrs Thomas says, but she's smiling a bit, 'to join her in the WVS.'

'Margaret Bevan's one of the nice ones,' Mr Thomas says. 'Your teacher is safe.'

'Yeah, but she won't fit in with the nice ones,' I say.

His forehead wrinkles like Dad's does when he's concentrating on the crossword. He waves his fork at me. 'Go on.'

'Nothing,' I say.

Ronnie sits up. 'My brother doesn't like Miss *Good*hew because she gave him the cane. Right across his pams.' He holds up his hands.

'Palms, Ronnie.' I cut into my Yorkshire pudding. 'It was nothing.'

'That sort of thing's never nothing,' Mr Thomas says. 'It's a weak adult who gets their power from hitting a child.'

I remember the sting of the birch on my hands. The shame of the tears I couldn't stop. Mr Thomas is right.

I scoop some gravy on to a piece of cabbage, thinking about it all and feeling lost. We're just finishing up when Ronnie sighs.

'Mr Thomas?' he says, a question in his voice. I get a worried feeling about what he's going to say. Mr Thomas puts down his knife and fork and leans across the table.

'Yes?'

'Why didn't you say grace?'

'Ronnie!' I splutter. A piece of cabbage flies out of my mouth on to the table. I pick it up, embarrassed. 'It's none of our business. And anyway, you should've had your eyes closed.'

Mr Thomas watches me for a second. I get the feeling he knows I was peeping too. He fixes his coal-black eyes on Ronnie.

'Davies up at Top Farm raised the cow, I grew the vegetables, Gwen cooked the meal.'

Ronnie frowns. 'Didn't God help at all?'

'Not that I can see.'

'Alun, please, not now,' Mrs Thomas says. 'Boys, finish your dinner. Then I'll tell you what you can do while –' she glances at her husband – 'I'm at chapel this evening.'

'Aren't you going, Uncle Alun?' Ronnie asks.

Uncle Alun? Where'd he get *that* from?

Mr Thomas smiles. 'Oh, I'm beyond redemption,' he says in his low, deep voice. He gets up from the table, kisses the top of Mrs Thomas's head and walks out of the back door.

CHAPTER SEVEN

SNAP

After washing up, Mrs Thomas passes me a mug of tea.

'Take it out to Alun, will you?' she says.

The back door is open and I can hear Mr Thomas grunting as he digs. I look at the steaming mug and then back at her. I don't want to but I go out anyway. I'm just over the doorstep when Ronnie calls her 'Aunty Gwen' again. I kick hard at a stone; it pings off the garden wall and hits a flowerpot. Good, I hope I've cracked it.

I walk around the side of the house to the vegetable plots. Mr Thomas leans on his spade, staring into space. He doesn't seem to know I'm there until I'm right next to him, holding out the mug. He nods a thank you but takes it without looking at me.

There are chickens scratching the ground in that little pen – four of them, all fat and fluffed up. Next to it, the wind moves the flowered roof of the air-raid shelter.

'Gwen,' Mr Thomas says.

'Pardon?'

'Gwen reckons a garden's not a garden without flowers.' He blows on his tea, then takes a drink.

'We've got a garden. People think London's all concrete and grey but it isn't. My nan's trying to grow some veg in case we get rationed but she's not very good at it. Not like my grandad, he had an allotment.' I stop. I can't believe I just told him all that.

'Hasn't he got it any more?' Mr Thomas asks.

'He died.'

'There's a lot of that about … and more coming.'

I push some soil around with my foot. 'Did you build it? The shelter, I mean.'

'I did.'

'It doesn't look like other ones I've seen.'

'That's because it's not from a kit.'

I've never heard of a *really home-made* air-raid shelter. It looks brilliant. I want to ask him about it – like how he made it, if he drew up plans first, how long it took – but then he might think I want to be here. I look at the rhubarb for a minute, then go back inside.

I glance up from a *Dandy* comic. The clock on the mantelpiece says ten past two. Usually, on a Sunday afternoon, I'd be helping Dad strip an engine or tidy his toolbox, getting mucky and laughing about how much Nan would complain. Or I'd be messing about with Duff. I wonder again where he's staying. If there's no school tomorrow I won't see him there either. I'm not going to miss lessons, but I do miss having my best mate next to me.

Through the open kitchen door, I can see Ronnie and Mrs Thomas at the table playing snap. She leans sideways and smiles at me. 'Want to play? I can deal you in after this game. It looks like your brother's going to win soon, anyway.'

Ronnie's pile of cards is huge next to her small one.

'I won all these, Jimmy!' He picks them up and waves them in the air. They fly out of his hand and fall all over the place. He jumps down, laughing as he picks them up.

'That's what happens when you let him win,' I say to Mrs Thomas. 'He gets silly.'

'She didn't let me win!' Ronnie shouts. Then he looks at her small pile of cards, still neatly stacked on the table. 'You didn't, did you, Aunty Gwen?'

She flashes me a look like she's annoyed, then turns back to him. 'Of course not, bach, I'm no match for you.'

Ronnie narrows his eyes at me. 'See?'

Idiot. I pick up the *Dandy* again. Mrs Thomas tells Ronnie to go and see what Mr Thomas is doing in the garden. She stands in the doorway. I lift the comic up in front of my face, like Mr Thomas did with his newspaper.

Her voice is quiet. 'Was there any need for that?'

I ignore her.

'Jimmy, please put the comic down so I can speak to you.'

I turn the page, not really seeing what's on it but pretending to be gripped by the latest adventures of Korky the Cat.

She sighs. 'I know this is hard for you, bach, you don't want to be here, you miss your family, but …'

I turn another page. She keeps on.

'If you're going to take it out on anyone, don't let it be your little brother. He's just trying to make the best of things – and he's only six.'

I want to scrunch the *Dandy* up into a ball and throw it, but I take a deep breath and put it down instead.

'I know how old he is, he's *my* brother.'

Just then, there's a knock on the front door. We look at each other for a second before she steps past me and out to the passage. I hear a boy's voice, and for one stupid second I think – I hope – it's Duff, but this voice is Welsh. I get up and put my head around the door frame. It's Ieuan, the lad from Sunday school. He sees me and waves. I nod my head once.

Mrs Thomas is speaking now. 'I'm sure he'd love to but … I don't know.' She sighs. 'He's only little and doesn't know his way around yet.'

'He'll be with me, Gwen. I'll look after him, I promise.'

She fiddles with the straps of her pinny. 'All right then, but you keep a close eye on him. Remember he's new. Don't let him wander off.'

She doesn't look at me as she passes on her way to the garden. Ieuan calls down the passage. 'I told Ronnie I'd show him a foxhole. You coming?'

I can't think why there'd be one of those round here but I'll do anything to get out of this house. Just as I'm walking towards the front door, Ronnie bounces past. 'Ieuan, can we really go now? Aunty Gwen says we can!' He grabs Ieuan's sleeve. 'Let's go!'

Mrs Thomas calls from the foot of the stairs. 'Have fun – be back for tea.'

*

It's so sunny out on the street I have to cover my eyes with my hand. We turn right. The tortoise is washing her windows. She stops as we go past.

'You children landed lucky when you came here, didn't you?'

Did we?

'Fresh air and lovely countryside. All slums in London, isn't it?'

I open my mouth to say something back but Ieuan shakes his head at me.

'You could be right, Mrs Maddock,' he says. 'The coal tips are particularly splendid at this time of year.'

I laugh so suddenly it comes out like a snort. She turns away and rubs furiously at the glass.

Ieuan grins. 'Take no notice, mun. I don't think she's ever seen an English person before, that's all.'

We walk along Heol Mabon until we join the hill they call the Bryn. We cross it and walk down a street called Heol Somethingelse. I couldn't say it if I tried.

A rough-haired black dog runs towards us, its ears flat against its head. Ieuan grins, bends over and smacks his hands on his thighs.

'Oh, you're coming too, are you?' he says. The dog reaches us and dances round, barking happily. It looks a bit old with its grey snout but it's acting like a puppy. Ieuan grins. 'This is Noble.'

Ronnie drops to his knees, laughing and spluttering as Noble licks his face.

'We need to go this way,' Ieuan says, waving his hand down the street towards a fence that leads on to sloping green fields. 'Noble will show us.'

The dog bounds off.

Someone's sitting on the fence, swinging their legs. As we get closer I see the someone is a girl. We get closer still and I can see exactly which girl it is. Worse luck.

Florence Campbell glares at me as she fiddles with the blue ribbon in her hair. She looks really different without the dirt.

I glare back.

'You never said *she* was coming.' I'm speaking to Ieuan but looking at her.

'Why wouldn't I come?' she says. 'I'm his sister.'

'You're *what*?' I laugh. I can't help it.

'She is,' Ieuan says. 'My mam says she's part of our family now.'

'Like us and Aunty Gwen and Uncle Alun!' Ronnie beams.

'Not really,' I say, but he takes no notice.

Ieuan looks from me to Florence as if he wants to say something, but he just climbs over the fence and holds out a hand to her. She takes it like she's a flaming princess or something, and steps down into the field. I don't know why she's making out she's all delicate; she was the best climber in our PT class. Even Miss Goodhew said she was like a rat up a drainpipe.

'Come on, Jimmy,' Ronnie says, putting his foot on the lowest panel. 'It's a foxhole! Don't you want to see a fox?'

'Don't be daft,' I say. They all stop to look at me. 'It's not that sort of foxhole, it's an army foxhole – a DFP – a defensive fighting position.' Ieuan isn't the only one around here who knows things.

But Ieuan scratches under his cap and looks a bit embarrassed. 'Err … this one isn't, Jimmy. It's a fox's *home*, a den.' He helps Ronnie over the top of the fence.

My cheeks burn. I might turn around and leave them to it.

But where would I go?

'You coming then, Jimmy?' Ieuan smiles. Then he whistles, and Noble takes a running leap, scrambles over the fence and races away up the mountain. Ieuan follows, Ronnie scampering at his side.

It's just Florence Campbell and me, on either side of the fence. She smirks. 'Who's the daft one now?'

Then she's off too.

CHAPTER EIGHT

THE FOXHOLE

By the time I catch up with them, Ronnie's wearing Ieuan's cap again. He's got it on backwards and looks a real fool.

'Look, Jimmy,' he says, 'Florence put it on me this way so I can see!'

I glance at her.

'Looks sweet, doesn't he?' she says, daring me with her eyes again.

'He looks –' I watch Ronnie, marching proudly up the slope with his little cowlick sticking out of the front of the cap – 'like Ronnie.'

Mountains are hot work. I take off my jumper and tie it round my waist. Ronnie sees me and does the same. He's talking to Ieuan and Florence like they're proper friends. He's saying something about bears and they laugh and laugh just like they did outside the chapel. If Ronnie's got bears muddled with foxes, he's in for one heck of a disappointment.

I fall back. It's like I'm on the outside, not quite a part of what's going on. I can hear Ieuan telling Ronnie and Florence about the trees and the flowers, the birds and other wild animals, how his grandad used to work on a farm in the next village.

I miss concrete.

Every few minutes one of them turns around: Ronnie to grin at me, Ieuan to wave me on, Florence to scowl like an angry cat. Noble mostly trots along with us but sometimes he races across the fields like a mad thing, his ears and tongue flapping about.

Ieuan leads us right, to a little wooden gate in the middle of a hedge; only it isn't a gate because you can't open it. It's an odd sort of step. Ronnie balances on the plank that's sticking out. I rush up to hold him around his middle in case he falls.

Ieuan smiles at me. Florence doesn't. Noble hops his front paws up on to the gate that's not a gate and Ronnie puts his arm around the dog's neck.

'See down there?' Ieuan points into the valley. 'That's the whole of Llanbryn, that is.'

Stuck on this side of the mountain are the rows and rows of houses we saw when we first got here. I try to work out which one is Heol Mabon but they all look the same. At the bottom is the railway station; there's a train at the platform puffing clouds of black smoke. It's facing towards England. My heart squeezes even more than it did yesterday. I just want to go home.

Ronnie looks back at me, his eyes bigger than ever. 'You can't do this in London, can you, Jimmy? You can't stand in one place and see the whole of it.'

'No, you can't,' I say quietly.

'London must be enormous,' Ieuan says.

'It's bigger than Wales, I expect,' Ronnie says. He looks out over the valley again and all three of us older ones laugh. Florence and me catch each other's eye and stop.

'What are those lumps?' Florence asks, pointing at the smaller black hills sitting on top of the mountains.

'Coal tips,' Ieuan says.

'Like a rubbish tip?'

'In a way. It's the stuff that comes out with the coal that isn't needed.'

'And is that the pit?' She points at the brick buildings and tall, thin chimneys. Huge metal structures stand next to them like giant Meccano.

'It is.' He looks at the pit the way Dad looks at an engine. 'I can't wait to get started down there.'

'Down the mine?' I can't keep the surprise out of my voice. Miss Williams said he was going to be a collier, but I didn't think anyone would *look forward* to being down there. In those small tunnels and darkness.

'Yeah, not that my mam's too happy about it – wanted me in the shop, see. To carry on the family tradition. But I can't spend the rest of my life weighing out butter for all the old dears, mun. I want to dig out coal, especially now there's a war on. I want to do my bit. Coal will fuel this war – railways, ships, factories, they all need it.'

Ronnie's giggling with Florence. 'He said "old dears".'

'What do you want to do then, Jimmy?' Ieuan asks.

Before I can answer, Ronnie says, 'He wants to be an engineer. Like our dad.'

'Dad's a mechanic, you nitwit.'

Ieuan smiles. 'Engineer or mechanic, both good jobs.' He scratches his head. 'My father always wanted to run the shop, take over from *his* father, was never interested in the pit.'

'Is your dad as nice as Phyllis?' Ronnie asks.

'He was,' Ieuan says, staring hard at the mine. 'He died when I was eight.'

Ronnie takes his hand and I find I don't mind.

I look out over the mountain. I've never seen countryside like this, not even in pictures. I expected to see green fields, but not chimneys puffing out smoke, and coal tips like black sand dunes.

'We going then or what?' Florence says. I don't think she likes me talking to her 'brother'.

Half an hour later, we're not too far from the top of the mountain when Ieuan stops and points to a small mound leading up to some bushes. 'It's in there.'

He tells Noble to sit and wait, which he does. We creep closer. It's like the entrance to a tiny cave, just big enough for a fox, I suppose. Roots hang down around it and the grass in front has been scratched away. Bare earth shows the way in.

'Do they live in there?' Ronnie whispers, getting on his knees for a closer look.

'Don't!' I pull him away by the shoulder. 'You don't know what's in there!'

'Oooh, what is it, Jimmy?' Florence laughs. 'The bogeyman? Are you scared?'

I hate her laughing at me. 'Don't be stupid, I just don't want him disturbing the foxes, that's all.'

'It's all right,' Ieuan says. 'They're only in there at breeding time. That's when they make tunnels and a bigger space to sleep and have their cubs.'

'Cubs?' Florence has a look on her face I've never seen before. Sort of soft.

'Yes, but there aren't any now,' Ieuan says, sounding sorry. 'You'd have to be here in the spring for that.'

Behind us, Noble growls and barks. He shoots off up the slope after a small grey blur.

'Rabbit,' Ieuan says. 'He loves a chase.'

'Oh no,' Florence moans. 'Don't let him catch it!'

Ieuan smiles at her. 'Don't worry, he never does.' Noble and the rabbit disappear into a hedgerow. 'I'd better fetch him back though.' He jogs off.

Florence looks at the foxhole. 'I hope I'm still here in the spring.'

Ronnie grins. 'Me too, I'd love to see fox babies!'

I stare at him, a small flame growing bigger and hotter inside me till it's a fire and I can't stop the words rushing out. 'Do you even know how long it is until spring? It's months and months – ages after Christmas even! Months away from Dad and Nan – is that what you want?'

Ronnie shakes his head, gulping back tears, and a voice in my head is telling me to shut up, but I keep going. 'Don't you know it's wicked to want a war to keep happening just so you can see a flaming baby fox?'

'I'm not wicked!' He's properly sobbing now, and the voice is telling me to give him a cuddle and say I'm sorry, but I can't make my arms move.

Florence steps right up to me. 'I'll tell you what's wicked.' She's standing on tiptoes, her face close to mine, and I'm shocked by how much she smells of soap. 'Making out *you* want to go home because of the war. Truth is you're just homesick … Missing your *mummy*, baby boy?'

A look flashes across her face like she's just remembered something and her mouth snaps shut. Ronnie flops down on the ground, covering his face with his arms.

'Look what you've done!' I rage at Florence.

'I didn't make him cry – you did!'

'He's *my* brother!'

'That doesn't mean you can be nasty to him—'

'Well, we all know why *you* want to stay here until the spring,' I say. She looks around nervously, as if she doesn't want Ieuan to hear, but he's at the top of the field. 'Even that muddy foxhole is better than *your* house. Why don't you go and live in there, Campbell? Why don't you get back in the *dirt*?'

She blinks like I've slapped her. I wait for the yells, the swear words – a thump even. But she just looks at me, and I can't believe it but there are tears in her eyes. And I don't know what to say, so I grab Ronnie by the arm and drag him away. He doesn't stop crying till we reach the fence.

CHAPTER NINE

FALLING

It's not long since breakfast but the sun's already hot. The valley's getting brighter; houses show themselves row by row and mist rises off the mountains like steam on washday. Nan always says washday is harder with boys' clothes to scrub. Well, thanks to Hitler and evacuation, it's a heck of a lot easier now.

I can't find Duff. I've been up and down the hill, looked in the swing park and on most of the streets. I even asked some people, but they don't know who Duff is so couldn't help. One of the houses had baskets of fruit and veg on the pavement outside so it must be Ieuan's mum's shop. Nan says shopkeepers know everything and everyone, but I'm not going in there. Not if Florence Campbell lives there now.

Three girls are playing hopscotch near the institute. One of them has plaits that bounce around as she hops. Lillian Baker. She might know where Duff is. As I get closer I can see the other girls are the ones who were talking Welsh in Sunday school yesterday.

'Hello, Jimmy,' Lillian says. 'Want to play?'

Play hopscotch with Lillian Baker and her new friends? Not likely. One of them says something in Welsh and the other one nods. So does Lillian.

She must be faking it; even a super-swot like her couldn't have learned another language in less than two days! But then she says something back, and it definitely isn't in English and all three of them giggle behind their hands.

That's it. I've had enough of this flaming village. Duff's nowhere to be found and Lillian flaming Baker's talking about me in Welsh!

I stomp off up the Bryn and across the streets to

the sloping field. But instead of going the way Ieuan showed us yesterday, I go a different one. My own way. Cutting left across the fields where he headed right, I come to a stream. I take off my shoes and socks and wade across. The water rushes around my ankles and my feet slip on the smooth stones.

The sun and the grass dry my bare feet as I walk towards a gate further up the mountain. I climb it, balancing on top and holding out my arms to feel a breeze through my shirt because it's sticking to me, like Ronnie's sticking to Mrs Thomas.

There's a huge tree across the field all on its own – a really good climbing one. It'll be cooler there. The sun is behind it and the branches are a fuzzy blur of brown and green.

I jump down and put my shoes and socks back on. About two-thirds of the way across the field, I come under the tree's huge shadow and look up. There are good knots in the trunk, making footholds and handholds for me. At the bottom, I launch myself; my fingers make claws to grip the bark and up I go. Reaching and climbing, reaching and climbing.

About halfway up, I stop to sit in a curve where the thickest branch meets the trunk. Something about being up here, hidden away from the world, makes me feel better. How can Lillian Baker and Florence Campbell fit in so easily when I just feel lost? Even Ronnie's getting on with it and making friends. He'd probably be fine here without me, in this horribly new place where everyone knows each other and being called Jones is somehow funny. But all I have is him, my daft little brother who forgave me straight away for being so horrible to him at the foxhole. I lean my head back and look up at the light flickering through the big, jaggedy-edged leaves. It'll be autumn soon and they'll start to fall, but I won't see it. The war will be over – people say it won't last till Christmas – and I'll be out of Wales and back in London by then. Please let it be soon.

I don't know how long I've been up here, but the sun's moved quite far across the sky. And I'm hungry. I suppose I'd better go. I twist around on the branch and slip backwards. Rough bark scratches the backs of my knees, my stomach's going to leave my body, and all I can see are branches and sky. My arms whirl and flap like a mad bird and I'm falling, falling. I reach out, grab hold of the tree and cling on, breathing hard, my heart pounding against the trunk. It's definitely time to get down.

I edge along the branch and hang like a monkey before dropping to the ground. I land awkwardly, my knees buckling, my arm flying out sideways as I try to save myself. My hand slides along the ground and into a gap in the tree trunk. It's a bit like the entrance to a wigwam and perhaps even wide enough for me to fit inside – not that I would try: small spaces make my head spin. I pull back and my fingers stroke something smooth and hard.

I rub the dirt off my scuffed hand, then grip the edges of the hollow and squint inside. It's quite dark and I can't make out much, but when my eyes start to adjust, a shape forms. On the ground just inside the tree is something round and dirty, about the size of a small football with three holes on one side. I reach in and hook my fingers through the holes to lift it out. Now it's in daylight I can see what it is.

And I feel like I'm slipping off the branch all over again.

A human skull.

My fingers are inside its eye sockets, touching the underside of the head – where the person's brain used to be.

I don't know how it got here, or whose it is, but I know it's real.

I try to shove it back inside the tree but my fingers shake and it falls to the ground, rolling into the long grass. I force myself to look. It lies there, watching me without eyes.

I don't want to put it back. I don't want to pick it up again.

I run.

From the top of the gate, I look back just once at the tree, the tree that has a skull lying next to it.

I keep running, down the mountain, not seeing where I'm going, just glad to be getting away.

I come to a footpath and race on, my lungs burning. I only stop when I come to a little stone wall. I lean on it while I get my breath back, my head down. Still panting, I look up to see rows of headstones. I've run to a graveyard. For a second I think I've run all the way down to the chapel, but I didn't see gravestones there. This is a church with a big, square tower like on a castle. It's huge, almost as tall as the Oxo Tower. It frowns down on me like it's trying to work out if I'm a sinner.

All those graves. All those bodies and bones. All those skulls.

I've never been afraid of graveyards. Back home, Duff and me used to play in the one near my house and try to guess what the bodies must have looked like from the dates on the headstones. I think about what's down below, in the graves in front of me – skulls and spines and ribcages. So many bones.

Bones like the one I just held.

But this wasn't the first time; there was that skull at school. Mr Lean passed it round in a science lesson last year. I touched my own face, feeling the bones under my skin and wondering what *my* skull looked like. Then Mr Lean got cross because Duff rolled up a piece of paper and made it look like the skull was having a ciggie. I laughed then, but I'm not laughing now.

The other skulls – the one at school, the ones in these graves – they're meant to be there. So how the heck does a skull end up inside a tree in the middle of a field? Who put it there? Is there a murderer in Llanbryn?

We were sent here to be safer. But I don't feel safe at all. I look around, half expecting to see a cloaked figure lurking behind one of the gravestones like in a spooky Saturday morning matinee. *Cut it out, Jimmy. You're sending yourself mad.*

'Who's there?'

The voice comes from nowhere and makes me jump. A man dressed in a grey suit steps out from behind a huge black cross. His shoes make a clip-clopping sound on the path. There's a white collar around his neck; he must be the vicar.

'You're not one of ours,' he says, coming over to the wall. 'Bit lost, is it?'

'No, I'm fine,' I say.

He smooths down his hair. 'From London, are you?'

'Yeah … I mean, yes. Islington.'

'Don't children take their hands out of their pockets when they speak to adults in Islington?'

I take mine out, feeling my cheeks burn hot.

'We've got a couple of you.' He says it like we're from another planet. 'Evacuees, isn't it? A boy and a girl. Duffy, they're called.'

'Duff's with you?' I say. Duff, who burps the alphabet and never says his prayers, is with a vicar! I try not to laugh.

The man's voice goes cold. 'Something funny, is there?'

'No, it's just … Never mind.'

The vicar smiles but I don't like the look of it. 'I didn't see you here at St Michael's yesterday, young man.'

The way he says it makes me feel like I'm being tested. 'We went to the chapel Sunday school, me and my little brother.'

'Better than nothing, I suppose. With whom are you billeted?'

I want to say it's none of his flipping business, but

I don't. 'We're with Mr and Mrs Thomas. Gwen and Alun.'

He doesn't even pretend to smile. 'Oh yes, I know them. It's a wonder you went to one of God's houses at all, then.'

'Mrs Thomas goes to chapel.'

The vicar pastes the false smile back on his face. 'Of course.' He leans closer; his teeth are long, grey and crooked, like the oldest gravestones behind him. 'But chapel is low down, see. Up here at St Michael's we're closer to God.' He looks up at the sky and smiles as if God is shining a light right down on him.

'I need to get back for my lunch,' I say, edging away.

It's like I haven't said anything at all because he carries on. 'Alun and Gwen Thomas …' He dips his head once and turns around. 'Now there's a pity.'

Why? Why is it a pity? What's wrong with the Thomases?

He walks off between the headstones and disappears into his church, his footsteps echoing like his words.

Not one of ours.

CHAPTER TEN

COW SOUP

Back in the kitchen of number twenty-one, Ronnie's getting spoons out of a drawer and laying them on the table. Mr Thomas washes his hands; he's scrubbing hard but his nails don't really get clean. Dad's hands are like that. Engine oil and coal dust must be sort of the same.

The whole house smells warm and peppery and sweet. Whatever Dad and Nan are having for lunch, it won't smell as nice as this; Nan's an awful cook. The vicar might think it's 'a pity' that we're here but at least it's somewhere with good nosh.

Mrs Thomas is stirring a big pan on the stove. I think she might tell me off for being out on my own so long but she just smiles and gives me that look again, getting the measure of me, taking me in. I wish she wouldn't.

Ronnie grins. 'We're having cow!'

'What?' I say.

'It's Welsh.' He points to the pan.

'Isn't everything?' I say, under my breath.

Except it wasn't under my breath enough. Mrs Thomas stares at me, her eyebrows raised. I look away. Flipping heck, why doesn't she just get cross, like a normal grown-up? Nan would.

Mr Thomas dries his hands on the tea towel and ruffles Ronnie's hair. '*Cawl.* Welsh stew. Lamb and vegetables.'

'So there's no cow in it, then?' Ronnie asks, sitting down.

'There's not even much sheep, I'm afraid,' Mrs Thomas says, bringing the pan to the table and dishing out the stew. She frowns down at it. 'I knew I should've used corned beef instead.'

'You wanted the boys to have proper Welsh cawl, Gwen,' Mr Thomas says, 'and you can't have cawl without lamb.'

She sighs as we sit down. 'I know … I've left the bones in for more flavour, anyway.'

'Bones?' I don't mean to say it, it just comes out. I must sound panicky because Mrs Thomas's voice is gentle when she says she'll make sure there are none in my bowl.

'I'll have them!' Ronnie says. 'I like sucking them, don't I, Jimmy?'

Normally, I'd fight him for them but today the idea makes me feel sick. Then another thought hits me – what if there are more bones in the tree? What if there's a whole skeleton or lots of skeletons or –

What if it's just a skull on its own? That might actually be worse. Because who puts a head in a tree?

I squash the meat with my spoon, just to be sure it's absolutely bone-free.

Mr Thomas doesn't say grace today, either.

'Where have you been, Jimmy?' Ronnie says, tearing a chunk off his bread and dipping it in the bowl.

'Out.' I blow on my spoon.

'Where?'

'Just out.'

'You didn't tell me you were going,' Mrs Thomas says. 'I like to know where you are. Keep you safe for your dad and nan.'

'I can keep myself safe.'

Ronnie starts talking to Mrs Thomas about Ieuan. Mr Thomas and me eat in silence. We're all sitting here, having our lunch as if this is normal. We're in another country that feels like another world, there's a big scary war on that no one seems to be talking about, and an hour ago I was standing under a tree holding a dead person's head.

Nothing about being here is normal.

When we've finished, Mr Thomas leans back in his chair. 'There might not have been much lamb but it was a tidy meal, Gwen.'

'Mine isn't tidy, I made crumbs,' Ronnie says, trying to sweep them into his hand but dropping them on the floor instead.

Mr and Mrs Thomas look at each other and laugh.

I don't like it; it's like a joke about my little brother that only they know. Until Mr Thomas explains.

'Round here, "tidy" means everything is just right.'

Blimey, even when Welsh people speak English it doesn't make sense.

Mrs Thomas leaves the table, gets a dustpan and brush from the cupboard under the sink and hands them to Ronnie. He looks at her.

'You made the mess, you clean the mess,' she says.

'All right, Aunty Gwen.' He crawls around under the table, banging the dustpan and brush against the chair legs.

'I saw Margaret Bevan this morning,' Mrs Thomas says from the pantry.

'Oh yes?' Mr Thomas lifts his legs for Ronnie.

'The collection money's gone missing from St Michael's.' She reappears with a big pudding bowl in her hands. 'They're calling it theft.'

'And who are *they*?'

'The usual. Hilda Ringrose for one.' She puts the bowl in the middle of the table.

'The gossips, then,' Mr Thomas says. 'The verger at

St Michael's is as old as the hills, she could have forgotten where she put it.'

'That's what I said, but Margaret says they're looking at the … err … *new arrivals*.'

New arrivals?

I stare at her. 'Us?'

'How very Christian-minded of them,' Mr Thomas mumbles. 'Blame the children.'

'But we only got here on Saturday!' I say. 'Not even a Campbell could work that fast!'

'What do you mean?' He fixes me with his dark eyes and I don't want to say what I mean so I just shrug and mumble that it doesn't matter.

'He means Florence,' Ronnie says.

Shut up, Ronnie.

'Florence?' Mrs Thomas asks. 'Isn't she Phyllis's girl?'

'Yes,' Ronnie says. 'She's Yi … Yi … oh, I can't say his name, but she's his sister now and she's really nice.'

'What did you mean then, Jimmy?' Mr Thomas presses, and I wish he'd just stop. I wish I'd never said that stupid thing.

'Her biggest brother went to jail.' Ronnie turns to Mr Thomas. 'He probably means that.'

Mrs Thomas looks cross. 'Well, *your* brother shouldn't have said that, Ronnie. It's wrong to tar everyone in a family with the same brush.'

But Mr Thomas smiles. 'What Gwen's trying to say is that some families have black sheep, that's all. Doesn't mean everyone in them will turn out the same.'

I want to say I know he's right. That even though Florence is from a whole flock of black sheep, I've never heard of her pilfering. Not once. But no words will come out.

Pudding is stewed apple and custard. Ronnie gets a bit down his chin and his tongue comes out to lick it off. I watch his mouth; how the jawbone moves so he can open and close it. It's like his skin isn't there and there's a skull eating stewed apple in the Thomases' kitchen. I have to shake my head to make it go away.

'You all right, boy?' Mr Thomas says.

I nod and fix my eyes on the sweet yellow mush in my bowl. Nothing in here looks like a skull.

CHAPTER ELEVEN

WELSH BOYS AND OLD FELLAS

Like yesterday, I slip out straight after breakfast. If I can find the vicarage where Duff is staying then everything will start to feel all right again. Duff always makes me laugh. If I tell him about the skull, maybe we can catch the murderer together. He isn't the best at working things out but there's no one else. And keeping it to myself is driving me mad. I left Mrs Thomas and Ronnie feeding the chickens. Ronnie loves them. Last night, before tea, he sat and watched them for ages.

Mrs Thomas said she's getting two more tomorrow and we can name them. Ronnie was silly with excitement but I told her we wouldn't be staying long enough for pets. And anyway, I don't think a stupid chicken can even *be* a pet.

Outside one house, a woman is scrubbing her front step. Some of the suds go on my shoes and I shake them off, splashing her arm.

'Careful!' she says, looking up. It's like she was going to smile but it fell off her face when she saw it was me. It's her – the woman in the purple hat from the institute, the one who frowned when Mrs Thomas chose us. Except she has a scarf tied on her head now and she doesn't look quite so uppity on her knees.

'Sorry,' I say. 'It was an accident.'

'Out of the way, you'll spread the dirt round!' She shoos me off.

I'm just crossing the Bryn when I see a group of boys coming down. One's waving and shouting to me. It's Duff. I stop and wait for them.

'This is Jimmy Travers,' Duff says to the others,

'the mate I told you about.'

The boys don't say anything; they just grunt and lift their chins. There are three of them, a scrawny, ratty-looking one with hair like straw – the boy from outside chapel – and two great big ones. Twins by the look of them but it's easy to tell the difference because one's got glasses. Duff points to them. 'Aled and Gareth.'

'All right?' I say.

'I'm Jack Evans,' says the scrawny one. 'My father's the Reverend Evans.'

I think he expects me to be impressed.

'What are you up to?' Duff asks.

'Nothing much.' I grind my shoe into the pavement.

'They're mitching.' Duff grins at the others.

'They're *what*?'

'Mitching. It's what they call bunking off round here.'

Jack sneers. 'Yeah, if you don't have to go to school, why should we?'

He takes a paper bag out of his pocket and offers it

round but not to me. They all take a butterscotch. The twins drop their wrappers on the pavement and crunch with their mouths open. Duff puts his sweet in his pocket and looks past me down the Bryn. I don't know what's going on. Back in London, he would have made sure I had one too.

There's no way I can tell him about the skull now, not with the others here. I search my brain for something to say. 'You learned any Welsh swear words yet, Duff?' As soon as we'd found out the train was set for Wales, he said that was his new ambition.

'Err, no, not yet.' Duff nods at a pointy-ended ball in Jack's hands. 'We're going down to the bottom field to kick this about.'

'Funny-looking football.'

'It's a rugby ball,' the one called Aled says. He looks like he wants to punch me in the face.

'I know what it is,' I say. 'I was kidding.'

Gareth taps the lid of his gas mask box and says nothing.

Duff points a thumb at Jack. 'I'm staying with Evs.'

'Yeah, you in a vicarage!' I laugh. I expect him to join in, make some joke about Holy Ghosts in the attic, but he doesn't.

'Got a problem with that?' scrawny Jack says. I bet he wouldn't be so mouthy without his big mates.

'Should I have?'

'Let's go.' Duff looks nervous. 'You coming, Jimmy?'

Before I get a chance to answer, Jack snarls, 'No. He's not.'

Duff and the Welsh boys walk down the hill. Jack turns. 'Oi, Jimmy, want to hear swear words in Welsh?' he shouts. 'Here, have this on me.' He yells something. Two words I can't understand but don't need to. It's obvious what they are. He laughs and the twins laugh with him.

So does Duff, and I know something between us has broken.

I kick a stone down the Bryn. Evacuation is a lie. They tell us we'll be safer in the country, but if it's a choice between getting my head kicked in by massive Welsh idiots or being bombed by Hitler, I'll risk the bombs. At least I'd be at home.

A dark-haired dog bolts around the corner, ears flapping, tongue lolling. It's Noble. I look around but I can't see Ieuan. Noble runs straight to me, tail wagging madly.

I stroke his head. 'Hello, boy. What are you doing out on your own, eh?'

He takes a few steps along the pavement, then turns as if he's waiting for me. I follow him to the fence, glad there's no Florence sitting on it today. He nudges a stick at my feet and woofs loudly.

'That's what you want, is it?' I can't help smiling as I pick up the stick and he leaps over the fence; it's good to have someone to play with, even if it's just a scruffy old dog.

A million throws later I think I'd rather be on my own but Noble could play fetch forever. And if I try to move away, he follows me, leaping and barking like mad.

I really don't want to take him back to Ieuan. Florence is bound to have told him what I said, and I don't know why, but that bothers me. I'll have to take Noble home and shove him through the door. I passed the shop before; it can't be too difficult to find it again.

*

These streets are the world's most boring maze. I walk up and down and backwards and forwards for ages. I'm sure I've seen these net curtains three times now. I need to ask someone.

On the next street down there're two old fellas sitting on stools on the pavement outside an open front door. As I get closer I can smell the tobacco from their pipes. Grandad had a pipe and he let me puff on it once. I coughed till I thought my eyeballs would fall out. We never told Nan.

The old fellas stop talking when they see me. Noble sniffs around their legs. One of them looks at him and says something in Welsh. It sounds like a question. Noble sits and gives the man his paw. I never knew animals could speak Welsh.

'All right, boy?' the other fella says to me. 'You look a bit lost.'

'I need to get the dog home,' I say. 'He's from the shop.'

'One of those evacuees, are you?'

'Yes.'

'London, isn't it?'

'Yes.'

'Bit different to round here. Must be quiet for you. You staying in the shop, are you? I heard Phyllis got herself an evacuee.'

'No,' I say, stepping away, hoping he'll get the hint. 'She's got a girl. Please can you tell me where the shop is?'

'Who are you billeted with then?'

I rock on my heels, trying to keep my patience.

'Gwen and Alun Thomas.'

'You hear that, Mal?' he says to the fella who's now scratching Noble behind the ears. 'Thomases have got themselves an evacuee.'

The one called Mal gets a funny look on his face, then says more things in Welsh. He talks fast and waves his hands about. The first fella seems to be trying to calm him down but I don't know what either of them is saying because it's all in Welsh now.

I don't care either; I just want to get this dog home.

'Look – never mind – I'll find it myself,' I say, tugging Noble by the scruff.

The first fella laughs. 'No need for that. That's the trouble with you city lot, always in a rush, you are! Go to the end of this street, then up, turn again and it's halfway along on the right. Got a big sign and baskets outside. You can't miss it.'

I tap my leg and Noble follows me. We walk away and the old fellas start their argument again. The only words I understand are *Alun* and *Gwen*.

CHAPTER TWELVE

D. HUGHES LTD

At last I know I'm on the right street. I see the baskets of fruit and veg, and Noble races off as we get near. The window is big and the paintwork over it is dark red. The name stands out in gold, bright and clean like the livery on a train:

D. Hughes Ltd

The D must stand for one of Ieuan's relatives, maybe his grandad. Noble noses his way through the door and I catch sight of Ieuan behind the till. I try to slip away but he sees me and then he sees Noble.

'Jimmy! Quick! Get him through to the back, mun,' he says. 'Mam'll go mad if she sees him in the shop!'

I don't need to do anything; Noble knows where to go. He slips through an opening in the counter, past Ieuan and into a back room that looks like a kitchen. I can just see his tail wagging as he drinks from his water bowl.

'He was out on his own.' I step inside and let the door close; the bell makes a tinkling noise.

'You didn't bring him back specially, did you?'

I nod, shoving my hands deep into my pockets.

'Well, that's good of you but you didn't need to. He goes out on his own all the time, mun. He'll probably be off again in five minutes.'

I feel stupid, but at least Ieuan is the same as he was yesterday, friendly and smiley. Maybe Florence didn't tell him about our row. The bell jingles, an old lady comes in, and I move out of the way.

On the shelves are Oxo cubes, Chivers jam, Bird's custard. I thought it would be different, that the labels and signs would all be in Welsh, but this could be a shop in Islington. I don't know if it makes me feel better or worse. There's a sign for Fry's Cocoa. When Mum was around to put us to bed, she used to make great big mugs of hot chocolate with that. A picture pops into my head: us laughing at Ronnie's frothy moustache. I blink it away.

The old lady asks for butter, then adds, 'Making a cake for my Frank, I am.' She looks at me like she expects me to know who her Frank is. 'Evacuee, is it?'

I nod.

'How's yours, Ieuan?' she says.

Ieuan breathes out really slowly before answering. 'If you mean *Florence*, she's very well, thank you. Mam's landed to have a girl about the place.'

Landed. Another word I don't understand here.

'Well, I'm sure she is but …' She leans over the counter and lowers her voice. 'I was just saying to Mrs Ringrose. Evacuees! From London, of all places! Why they couldn't send us some from Cardiff I'll never know. Now don't get me wrong, I *sympathise*, but we've barely enough for ourselves in this village without sharing it with waifs and strays.'

He weighs out the butter without looking at her. 'It doesn't matter where they come from. If we can help, then we should help.'

'Oh, of course, that's why I'm on the Welcome Party Committee –' she smirks – 'but we know where we are with our own, don't we? What with the collection money pinched from St Michael's. It's never happened before.'

'What, never?' He winks at me. 'Did you know that, Jimmy? You've arrived in a sainted land, mun.'

She makes a face like she's sucking a lemon.

I hear laughing coming from the kitchen. Ieuan must see me looking because he stops wrapping the butter and smiles. 'Mam's showing Florence how to make Welsh cakes.' There's a loud squeal and more laughing. Ieuan shakes his head and sighs. 'No idea what's so funny about flour and currants myself.'

While Ieuan takes the old lady's money, I listen to the happy sounds coming from the kitchen. Florence Campbell never laughed in London. Here she does it all the time – outside chapel, up the mountain – and

I don't know what I thought her laugh would be like but I'm a bit surprised it's nice-sounding and so … *girly*.

The old lady leaves.

'Ignore her,' Ieuan says, wiping his hands on his apron. 'Some people have no idea about the world outside this valley. Never left Llanbryn, mun. So, how's Ronnie? Feeling any better, is he?'

'Pardon?'

'His stomach ache – yesterday up at the foxhole – Florence said that's why you left so quick.'

'Oh,' I say, cottoning on. 'Yeah, he's, erm, fine now. Thanks.'

'Florence!' Ieuan calls back into the kitchen. 'Jimmy's here. He said Ronnie's fine.'

Florence appears in the doorway; her face is streaked with flour and her thick hair is powdered white. It looks like one of those wigs from the olden days. She watches me but says nothing.

'You stand by here and mind the shop a minute while I go and tell Mam about an order,' he says to her. Wiping her face, Florence steps behind the counter. I turn and pretend to be interested in a sign that says *Brasso – The New Liquid Metal Polish*. I'm sure I feel her eyes boring into me like a drill. I can't blame her. What I said to her at the foxhole was horrible.

So I do something that surprises even me. I turn to Florence, look her right in those hard-staring eyes and say:

'I'm sorry. For what I said.'

She shrugs. 'I'm used to it.'

I know this is true. I think about school and the way the others were always saying things like that to her. I never thought I'd be one of them. They called her names or waved their hands under their noses when she was near. I never did it; Nan always told me it wasn't Florence's fault she was dirty. But I never stood up for her either. I just used to keep out of it and make sure she never sat next to me.

'You can keep it though,' she says.

'Keep what?'

'Your apology. I don't want it.'

Now it's my turn to feel like I've been slapped in the face.

'Know why?' She's daring me again. I shake my head – even if I knew what to say I don't think anything would come out. 'Because I expected better from you, Jimmy Travers. I thought you were different.'

I don't know what to say or what to do, because she's right. *I* expected better of me. *I* thought I was different.

So I leave. Flaming evacuation. Flaming Wales. Making me say things I'd never normally say.

Changing me.

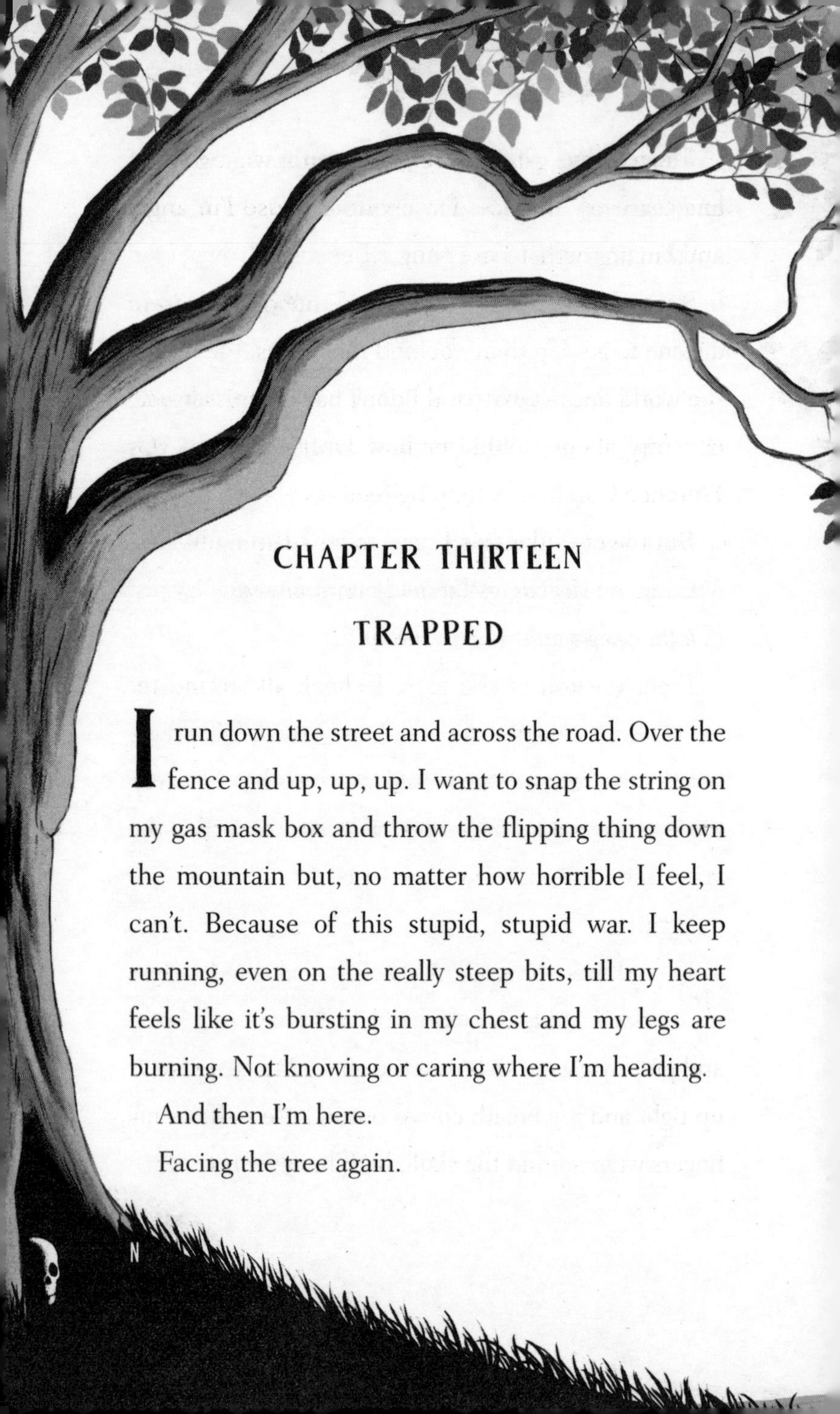

CHAPTER THIRTEEN
TRAPPED

I run down the street and across the road. Over the fence and up, up, up. I want to snap the string on my gas mask box and throw the flipping thing down the mountain but, no matter how horrible I feel, I can't. Because of this stupid, stupid war. I keep running, even on the really steep bits, till my heart feels like it's bursting in my chest and my legs are burning. Not knowing or caring where I'm heading.

And then I'm here.

Facing the tree again.

I lean on the gate to catch my breath, wiping sweat and tears off my face. I'm crying because I'm angry and I'm angry that I'm crying.

Across the field, the tree reminds me that I do have a place to go. Up there, behind the leaves, the rest of the world doesn't exist and I don't have to miss home, or worry about Ronnie or how Duff's changed. Or Florence Campbell's flipping feelings.

But to get to the tree I have to pass the skull.

Come on, Jimmy, it doesn't have to be scary; it's just like the one in your science lesson.

From the top of the gate, I check all around for people but I can't see anyone. I cross the field and my heart starts pounding. I hold my breath and creep towards the spot where I left it. A breeze ruffles the grass under the tree and there it is.

Waiting.

I stand over the skull. My hands shake and I close my eyes and suddenly I can't look. But I have to. I kneel and put my gas mask box in the grass. My face screws up tight and my breath comes out in little puffs as my fingers wrap around the skull, both hands this time.

It's only bone. Nothing to be scared of.

Questions pour into my mind like someone turned on a tap. What the heck happened? How long has it been here? And who did it? I do know one thing though: it really *isn't* that different to the one in my science lesson.

Up in the tree, behind the leaves, is the best place to think; my hide-away-from-the-world place. I can't climb and hold the skull though. I look at my gas mask box; the skull would easily fit in there. I put the gas mask in the hollow, the skull in the box, and climb. I'm fast, sitting on the branch before you can say Jack Robinson.

I take out the skull and hold it in front of me. I run my fingers over it and feel a small dent, a crack in the bone just at the back of the head.

'What happened to you?' I whisper. 'Who are you?'

And all of a sudden I realise that's what I need to do. This used to be someone.

And I'm going to find out who.

'Jimmy?'

The voice makes me jump and I peer down through

the branches to see Ronnie squinting up at me, his hand over his forehead like the sun's in his eyes.

'What do you want?'

'Aunty Gwen sent me to get you, it's nearly dinner-time.'

'What?' *How long have I been here?* Then I remember that in Llanbryn dinner means lunch. 'How did you know where I was?'

'I saw your legs hanging down.'

'But how did you know I was on the mountain?'

'I saw Duff and he said you came this way so I looked for you.'

If Ronnie can find me so could Duff – and those boys. They're the last people I want nosing around. Because, after what happened this morning, I know I can't tell Duff anything.

'Hurry up,' he says. 'I wasn't supposed to go further than the end of the street.'

'Ronnie, Mrs Thomas will be frantic! You know how she fusses.' I sneak a look at the skull, then back at Ronnie. 'You go back and I'll follow you in a minute.'

'Why can't we go together?'

'Just do as you're told.'

He gets a smiley look in his eye – it's the same one he had at the chapel when he shouted out 'Aunty Gwen'. 'I'll wait for you,' he says, folding his arms. 'Then I can see what's in your hand.'

Little git! He's got me trapped.

'There's nothing in my hand,' I say, turning so the skull's behind my back.

'Show me then.'

I show him one at a time, carefully manoeuvring the skull from hand to hand like a really bad magician. But he's not fooled.

'I'm not going without you,' he says.

'Suit yourself.'

I tuck the skull out of sight in my lap and lean back against the trunk again.

A little voice floats up from the ground. 'Is it a football?'

'No, just go away.'

'A rugby ball?'

He's definitely seen something. 'It's nothing, Ronnie.'

'Come down then. I want my dinner.'

'Lunch.'

'Dinner.'

This could go on all day … and now he's started jiggling about, his hands over the front of his shorts. I know that little dance.

'Need a wee?' I ask.

'No.'

I know he's lying. I'm just about to start talking about rivers and waterfalls and long drinks of water when a gunshot cracks the air a few fields away. I rock on the branch, feel the skull leave my hand, swipe the air with desperate fingers, but it falls and lands at my little brother's feet.

He makes no sound; just stands there staring at it. Like he's frozen. I almost fall out of the tree in my scramble to get down. I grab the skull. Ronnie's eyes are fixed on me now but it's like he isn't seeing me. He steps back, shaking his head. Oh heck, a dark, damp patch is spreading over his shorts. I put my arm out to him but he backs even further away. I look at the skull in my hand, then I make a parting in the long grass at the bottom of the tree and hide it there.

'Come on,' I say. 'Let's get you cleaned up. There's a stream down there, we can wash out your wet things. You can wear my shirt, it'll cover you right up.'

He seems to snap awake. 'All right, Jimmy,' he says, but his eyes are still blank.

I walk him to the stream, take off my shirt and slip it over his. We don't say anything while I swill his underpants and shorts in the water. I hang them on a bush to dry and we sit for a while.

'Is it really a skull, Jimmy?' Ronnie says.

I look at him, at his big doe eyes. But there's no point lying to him now; he might be six and daft but he isn't *stupid*.

'Yeah,' I say. 'It is.'

'Of a person?'

'I think so.' I turn to face the tree. 'I'm going to put it back.'

'Where?' He looks terrified. 'In its grave?'

I suppose, in a way, the tree is a grave and I wonder

if I should have taken it out at all. 'No. The tree. I'm putting it back and you can't tell anyone it's there.'

'Why?'

'Because I said so.'

'You sound like Nan.'

'Look, I found it so it's my secret and you can't tell another person's secret, especially not to a grown-up. They spoil things.'

They do. They think they know everything but all they do is leave or make wars or send their children away.

'Can I tell Ieuan then? Or Florence? They aren't grown-ups.'

'No.' I feel his clothes, they're still quite damp but they'll just have to finish drying while we walk. 'We don't know who we can trust and, anyway, it's just you and me here, Ronnie.'

'It isn't just us.'

It's best to ignore him now. 'Come on. Then we can go back for lunch.'

'Dinner.'

'Ronnie, I'm not doing this again. Move.'

'I'm not coming.' He pulls at some grass, waggling his fingers and letting it fall over his bare legs.

I grab his clothes off the bush. 'All right, you stay here. Watch out for Welsh snakes though – one might come and bite you on the backside.'

He's up and after me like a shot.

CHAPTER FOURTEEN

A GREAT RIGHT HOOK

Ronnie's still a bit damp as we walk to Heol Mabon, back in our own clothes now, our gas mask boxes bumping against us as usual. He's still in a daze so we don't walk fast, even though we're both starving. We're almost there when Duff and Jack come round the corner.

'All right?' I try to keep moving but they get in the way.

'All right?' Duff says.

Jack looks at Ronnie in a way I don't like. 'Why

are your shorts wet?'

'He fell in a stream,' I say, standing up really straight so Jack will feel even smaller.

'Fell in a stream?' His face is all twisted up like he's trying to be tough but he just looks rattier than ever.

Ronnie puts his head down and grabs my hand.

'You sure he didn't pee himself?' Jack says.

Before I can deny it, Ronnie gives the game away by bursting into tears. Jack laughs. I look at Duff, who just shrugs. Not long ago he would have been on our side.

'So you did then?' Jack leans down to Ronnie. He doesn't have to lean very far.

'Shut it!' I say, shoving Jack hard on the shoulder.

He staggers back. 'You'll wish you hadn't done that, vaccie.'

'Get lost.' I try to drag Ronnie away but he's stuck to the spot.

'Is that what you lot do? Just pee wherever you like?' Jack sneers. 'Filthy vaccies. I saw you talking to that Campbell shunk outside the chapel the other day too. She's not fooling anyone with her clean dress, is she, Duff?'

I don't know what a shunk is but I can guess. Duff must have told Jack that Florence is usually dirty and, I don't know why, but it makes me even angrier.

'If vaccies are so filthy, why are you mates with one?' I say.

'Not all of you are bad.' Jack puts an arm around Duff's shoulder. 'Anyway, he's one of us now.'

Duff grinds his shoe into the pavement.

Jack's right in Ronnie's face again. 'Did you pee yourself, little vaccie?'

I grab the back of Jack's tank top and pull him away but before I can land a punch—

BAM!

A fist flies from nowhere into the side of Jack's face. He crashes hard on to the pavement with a noise that sounds like the wind's been knocked out of him.

'She broke my jaw,' he mumbles, holding his cheek.

She?

'You wouldn't be able to speak if I'd done your jaw.' Florence Campbell stands over him, fist up, ready for a second blow. 'Now clear off before I give you another.'

Jack gets to his feet, all wobbly. Duff looks as stunned as me as he helps him up. When Jack moves his hand from his face, his mouth is bleeding.

'She's not right in the head,' he says, grabbing Duff and pulling him up the hill.

Florence gives Ronnie a hanky. 'You all right?' she says. He wipes his cheeks, blows his nose and goes to give it back. She pulls a face. 'Keep it.'

'Thanks, Florence,' Ronnie says. He points at a little brown paper parcel in her hand. 'What you got?'

Florence holds it up. 'Welsh cakes. Phyllis asked me to take some to your house. Want to walk together, Ronnie?'

She holds out her hand and he takes it. I follow – again. They chat as they walk. When we turn into Heol Mabon, Florence looks round at me and actually smiles. Not a smirk or a sneer but a real, proper smile. So I smile back. Ronnie lets go of her and races off to number twenty-one. I catch up with Florence.

She looks at me sideways. 'All right?'

I nod. 'You've got a great right hook.'

'Thanks,' she says, making her hand into a fist again and holding it up in front of her like a trophy. 'You have to with a family like mine.'

She keeps looking at her hand, which isn't a fist any more.

'I really am sorry for what I said about your house,' I say.

She sighs. 'But you still said it.'

'Yeah.' I feel about two inches high.

She steps in front of me and folds her arms. 'But I've thought about it and I *will* accept your apology.'

'Oh … good.' And I mean it; I do feel glad. We're at the Thomases' open front door now. 'Florence?'

She looks at me. Her eyes are bright blue, like Mrs Thomas's.

'Why didn't you tell Ieuan what I said?'

She fiddles with her hair ribbon and a tiny bit of flour drops on to her shoulder. 'Because I was ashamed.'

'What did you have to be ashamed of? I was the idiot, picking a fight.'

'I didn't want Ieuan to know about my house. Being a Campbell's a bad thing, everyone knows it. Everyone back in Islington. But here I can be –' she shrugs – 'I don't know ... *different*.'

I think of what Mr Thomas said about black sheep. There's nothing I can say.

Ronnie runs down the passage towards us shouting about Welsh cakes. Florence grins and chases him back through the house.

She's different all right.

Mr Thomas is already eating a Welsh cake when I go in the kitchen. 'Try one of these, boy,' he says to me, holding the opened parcel. 'Almost as good as Gwen's.'

Welsh cakes aren't like any cake I've ever seen. They're round, spotted things, a bit like flat scones with sugar on. I take one and poke at it. I think the spots are currants.

Mr Thomas looks at Florence. 'You Phyllis's girl then?'

'Yes.' She looks around in a really nosy way.

'She's Florence,' says Ronnie.

'Nice lady, Phyllis,' Mr Thomas says.

Florence nods, biting into a Welsh cake.

Mrs Thomas comes in from the garden and puts the wash basket on the floor. 'Oh, you're back! Thank goodness! Where have you been? It's long past dinner-time.' She starts folding the washing, flapping the towels really fast.

'Late, are you?' Mr Thomas frowns, his eyes fixed on Ronnie and me. 'Don't worry your aunty. She's got enough to do with all the extra washing.'

'Well, they're back now,' she says. 'That's the main thing.' I don't know why she's so worried. Nan let us roam all over the place, as long as we were home for tea. And Mum never seemed to care where we were, teatime or not. So I don't see what Mrs Thomas thinks gives her the right to.

Mrs Thomas says that Ronnie and me have to eat our luncheon meat sandwiches before we have any more Welsh cakes. Mr Thomas puts the kettle on. We all sit at the table and Florence talks too much; about evacuation and living in a shop and how much she likes it in Llanbryn.

Mrs Thomas is clearing the plates when Ronnie says, 'Florence is a boxer!'

'Pardon?' the Thomases say together.

Florence fiddles with her ribbon and says nothing.

'It was Jack Evans,' I start. 'The vicar's son.'

It's like a dark cloud has drifted over Mr Thomas's face; his eyebrows scrunch down over his coal-black eyes. 'I know who he is.'

Mrs Thomas watches him like a nervous bird; I haven't seen them like this before. I nudge Florence but she just looks at the table. Ronnie's no better. Why does he always have to let the cat out of the bag and leave me to explain?

'Ronnie and me were coming back down from the mountain and he fell in the stream.' Mrs Thomas jumps up to feel his shirt. 'He's fine. It was only his shorts and … erm … underwear.' My cheeks burn. I look anywhere but at Florence. 'I tried to dry them on a bush. But we bumped into Jack and Duff, and Jack called us filthy vaccies and frightened Ronnie, but before I could do anything Florence was there.'

'And she did what exactly?' says Mrs Thomas.

'Gave him a proper belter.'

'Florence! Whatever would your mother say?'

Florence glances at me.

'He deserved it,' I say. Florence looks down at her plate and smiles. 'Anyway, Ronnie's fine now. We looked after him.'

'They did, Aunty Gwen,' Ronnie says.

Mr Thomas watches us all like he's seeing a film, like he's not really part of the conversation any more.

Mrs Thomas leans over and strokes Ronnie's head. 'I knew Jack Evans would be the one to cause problems with evacuees, didn't I say that to you, Alun? Gets away with murder, he does.'

I think again of the skull and how there might be a real murderer in Llanbryn.

'I'm going up to that vicarage and—'

'Leave it, love,' Mr Thomas says. 'The children have sorted it out themselves. The less we have to do with that family the better.'

Mrs Thomas sighs. 'I suppose you're right.' She

turns to us. 'But boys – you need to avoid him if you can. He's nothing but a bully.' She pats Ronnie's legs. 'Do you know what, I think these shorts are still a bit damp, bach. Let's get you changed before you catch a chill.'

'He's *fine*,' I say. 'I took care of him.'

She bustles him off upstairs anyway.

Mr Thomas gets up too. 'Nice to meet you, Flossie.'

He leaves too, taking the dark cloud with him through the house. The parlour door bangs shut.

'Who's Flossie?' I ask.

'Me, I suppose.' She grins but it quickly turns to a frown. 'Do you think he's cross with me?'

'Not if he's giving you a nickname.'

It's not her causing his bad mood. There's something else, and it's got to do with Jack Evans's family. I'm sure of it.

CHAPTER FIFTEEN

THE WELCOME PARTY

'I told you there'd be red pop,' I say. 'Now you can stop going on about it.'

Ronnie had been fretting all the way to the institute that there might only be green pop, which he didn't really like, but would have to drink because it was better than no pop at all. He shouldn't have worried. Phyllis's donation to the welcome party is about twenty bottles of the stuff.

I never thought I'd see Florence in a party dress. She keeps running her hands over the front of it and telling me it's the same colour blue as her ribbon. I don't know what to say so I just smile and nod.

The hall is laid out with tables made into a big U shape. Plates and plates of food sit on flowery table-cloths. Sandwiches, biscuits, Welsh cakes, jam tarts, lemon curd tarts, pop, cordial and – best of all – wobbling jellies and pink blancmange rabbits. Above the platform, a gigantic banner reads *LLANBRYN WELCOMES ISLINGTON EVACUEES*.

Mrs Evans and another woman – the rude old lady from the shop – buzz around like bossy wasps. Each table has the same food and drink on it, repeating and repeating all around the U shape like when a cartoon character runs and it's just the same stuff going past in the background.

Ronnie points to some egg sandwiches and jam tarts. 'Are those the ones we made, Aunty Gwen?'

Mrs Thomas nods but before she can say anything, Mrs Evans stops and spins around. 'Gwen Thomas, did I hear correctly? You allowed this boy to make food for the party?'

'Yes.' Her mouth and eyes have gone small and tight, like she's holding something in. 'Ronnie helped me weigh out the flour—'

'And I put the jam in, didn't I, Aunty Gwen? I *plopped* –' he makes a dropping action with his hand – 'it all in. Forty times.'

'*Plopped*, you say?' Mrs Evans's lips curl like he said a rude word. She starts to walk away. 'I hope he washed his hands.'

Mrs Thomas glares after her. 'One of these days I swear I'm going to …'

Phyllis puts a hand on her arm. 'Ignore her. She's just jealous because her pastry's like concrete. At least we don't have to put up with Hilda Ringrose too. She's away visiting her John. He's got a day off training, so she told me *five times* in the – Oh my goodness! What on earth happened to him?'

Jack, Duff and the twins are coming in. The left side of Jack's face is a bluish-purple. He keeps trying to cover it with his hand but you can't miss it.

'Fell over playing British Bulldog,' the old lady says from behind a tower of paper cups. 'Poor lamb.' She moves off, setting out the cups on the tables as she goes.

Mrs Thomas stares at Florence.

'It looks worse than it is,' I mutter, glad that Phyllis now seems more interested in rearranging the pop bottles.

I pull Florence away from the grown-ups and whisper, 'He hasn't told on you. What's his game?'

'Isn't it obvious?' she asks. I shake my head and she rolls her eyes. 'He can't admit to being *hit by a girl*, can he? So he makes up a story, but you can bet he won't let this rest. This won't be the end of it.'

The way Jack and the twins are looking at us now, I'm sure she's right.

Florence goes to help Phyllis.

Ronnie skips up to me. 'I like the hall like this. It's much better than when we got off the train.'

Before I can answer, a tall man walks over. It's the doctor who took all the Turners at the institute.

'Well, hello. You must be Gwen and Alun's evacuees.' He holds out a hand to me, which I shake, and then to Ronnie. He pretends my brother's grip is so strong that he has broken fingers. Ronnie thinks it's hilarious.

'We have so many I haven't learned all their names yet,' he laughs. 'But they're settling well. Been running around our garden like happy little savages.'

The Turner children live in a flat back home; staying with the doctor must be like having their own Highbury Fields.

Mr Bevan booms from the middle of the hall to say there'll be party games before food. Mrs Bevan plays the piano for musical statues. When the music stops Ronnie's hopping on one leg. Mr Bevan sees him but declares it a practice run.

Jack glares at Ronnie. 'Hey. That's not fair! *They're* getting special treatment again.'

'Now, now,' Mr Bevan says, 'we have to give the little ones a chance.'

'I'll give Jack Evans some special treatment if he doesn't watch his mouth,' Florence says under her breath.

Pin the tail on the donkey and blind man's buff are

next. Then, at last, they let us sit down to eat.

I tap Ronnie's hand to stop him picking up the edges of the sandwiches to see what's in them. Florence says she'll take a little nibble of them for him to check if they're the kind he wants. She says important people have food tasters to check their meals aren't poisoned and you can never be too careful. I tuck into a meat paste sandwich, wondering where she gets these ideas.

Lillian Baker's on the next table, saying 'please' and 'thank you' really loud in Welsh.

'What's she on about?' Florence says, stuffing a pink wafer into her mouth.

'Showing off, as usual,' I say.

Florence does a mime of someone throwing up.

Jack's across the hall, his plate piled so high I can just about see his ratty face over the top of it all. The bruise shines out good and proper though. He's lifting one of Ronnie's jam tarts to his mouth when his mother grabs his arm. She mutters something in his ear and he drops it like it really is poisoned.

Luckily, Ronnie's too busy trying to look at his own top lip to notice. I know what he's doing. 'Yes, you have got a red pop moustache,' I say.

'I'm like Mr Bevan!' he grins. 'I'll show him after tea.'

When we're all full to bursting, Mr Bevan says we're going to play musical chairs. Some grown-ups bring the chairs around to the centre of the hall, while others start clearing the tables. Two women chat as they take our plates.

'Did you hear what was found on the mountain?' one of them says.

My stomach flips over backwards. What if someone else has seen the skull?

'A Red Cross collection tin,' she says, and my head whooshes with the relief of it. 'Empty. Went missing from the post office counter, it did. Dai was on his way down from work and there it was, stuffed under a hedge. Saw the red on it, he did.'

Florence nudges my arm. 'You all right? Looks like you've seen a ghost.'

I nod.

'Been a lot of thieving around here lately,' the other woman says. 'We all need to watch out.' She moves to the next table. 'I don't mean all of them are bad. Or else I wouldn't be here, would I? But Ruth Evans told me her husband saw one of them –' she nods in my direction – 'lurking outside St Michael's, all shifty-like. And we all know that's where this started, don't we?'

'The collection money.' The other woman makes no secret of staring right at us. 'Well, if the reverend says so, it must be true.'

'Last call for musical chairs!' Mr Bevan booms.

Florence and Ronnie find chairs and I sit as far from them as possible. The music starts and off we go. Round and round the outside. Straight away, I deliberately lose and go to sit on the edge of the stage. If this is a welcome party, I don't feel very welcome at all.

CHAPTER SIXTEEN

SKULLS AND SKELINGTONS

Ronnie's screams wake me.

I catch the odd word in the babble – *skull, bones*. I stretch my arms out and feel around to find him in the blackness. There he is. Shaking his shoulder with my free hand, I whisper that it's me, that he's having a bad dream. I slip down on to his mattress and hold him tight until he stops crying and his breaths are normal again.

'Skulls and skelingtons were coming to get me,' he splutters.

'There aren't any skulls or skeletons here,' I whisper, flicking on the bedside lamp. We both blink at the brightness.

'There are on the mountain,' he says.

'Yes, but not here. I've got you. And the skull is just a bone. It can't hurt us. Now settle down before Mrs Thomas comes in like she did before.'

He fiddles with the end of my sleeve. 'Calling her Mrs Thomas is like living with a teacher.'

'It's not that much different though, is it? With them getting paid and everything.'

'What?'

'Nan told us, don't you remember?' He shakes his head so I carry on. 'People who take in evacuees get money off the government, to help feed us and get us new shoes and things like that.'

'Oh,' Ronnie says. His eyes look a bit watery again. I let him tug at my pyjama button. His voice is even more of a whisper now. 'Do you think Aunty Gwen and Uncle Alun only have us because they get money?'

I think about it for a minute. 'No, no I don't.'

'So they like us?'

'I think they do.'

I realise I'm telling the truth. It isn't just something to stop him worrying. When Mrs Thomas changed her mind and took us both that day at the institute, it wasn't for more money.

Ronnie flops across my lap, elbows on the mattress, chin in his hands. He waggles his legs in the air. When he was born, Dad put him on me, except he was facing up then. He was squashy and dark pink and kept opening his mouth like a fish. Mum said he was trying to smile at me. Knowing Ronnie, he probably was.

'I think you should tell Florence about the skull,' he says, reaching for his Dinky van and driving it along the edge of the mattress. 'She's nice now. Much nicer than she was in London.'

She is, but I don't say so.

'And she's clever,' he goes on. 'She could help us find out where it came from.'

'*Us?* Ronnie, you wet your pants!'

He drives his van on to the carpet. 'Well, you're a pig-face.'

I push him off me and climb back into bed. He's right about one thing though; Florence does get a lot of answers right at school. Perhaps she *is* clever. And I need to know what happened. It would be good to talk to someone else about it, investigate more, make plans. I think Florence might be good at that. But can I trust her?

'Can I get in with you?' Ronnie asks.

'I suppose. But wet the bed and you're for it.'

My mattress dips as he climbs in. He takes my arm and pulls it round him.

'Try to think about nice things,' I say.

'All right,' he says, surprisingly fast. 'I'm going to think about Florence punching that skinny Welsh boy.'

CHAPTER SEVENTEEN

BACON AND OATS

We've hardly finished our breakfast porridge when there's a hammering at the front door. Mrs Thomas jumps out of her chair, knocks over the milk jug and hops about like she doesn't know what to do next. Mr Thomas is having a lie-in so we're meant to be quiet.

'I'll clean it up, Aunty Gwen,' Ronnie says. Little goody-goody.

'Thanks, bach,' she says, and rushes to the door.

Ronnie gets a cloth and makes such a botch of

mopping up the milk I take it off him and do it myself. The person at the door is a girl – a loud girl with a London accent. Ronnie and me look at each other and say at the same time: 'Florence!'

'You can tell her *what you found*,' he says. He tries to wink but only manages to blink like a simpleton.

'Shh, Ronnie,' I say. 'Not now.'

Mrs Thomas brings Florence through the house and into the kitchen, presenting her as if she's a wonderful surprise. 'A visitor for you, boys,' she says, taking the cloth. She winks, and mouths 'Thank you' to me. I look away.

'Hello, Florence!' If Ronnie smiled any wider he'd crack his daft face. Florence grins back at him.

'Have you had breakfast?' Mrs Thomas asks her. I'm a bit surprised. She said there were hardly any oats left.

'Yes, thank you, Mrs Thomas,' Florence says. 'Me and Ieuan had toast and jam.'

'Call me Gwen, cariad.'

Ronnie sneaks a sly smile at me. 'There's no need

for mister and missus in this house. That's what Uncle Alun says.' He pulls Florence by the hand. 'Come and see the chickens. Aunty Gwen got two new ones yesterday and one is all mine. I named her Dorothy.'

'But it's your turn to do the dishes,' I say.

Ronnie gives Mrs Thomas his best doe eyes, the ones Mum used to fall for. She laughs. 'Five minutes – and then dishes! But keep the noise down, mind.'

Ronnie and Florence walk out, still holding hands. I go to follow them.

'You going too, Jimmy?' Mrs Thomas says. 'That's nice. You can think about what to call your chicken.'

'Chickens don't need names,' I say. 'They just need to taste nice.'

'Oh, Jimmy, why can't you …' But she doesn't finish, just sighs and wipes her forehead with the back of her hand. I stomp out of the door. I know it was a stupid thing to say, no one's going to eat them, but I wish she'd stop pretending this is our home.

Ronnie and Florence are in the coop, letting the birds peck all around them. Florence is giggling and stroking the big white one that Mrs Thomas says is mine. She looks up.

'She's lovely, Jimmy.'

'She's a chicken.'

Florence pulls a face and turns back to the bird. 'Well, I think you're beautiful. Don't you listen to that Jimmy – he's a silly boy. You're like a big fluffy snowball … Ooh, that's a good name for you.'

Ronnie giggles too. 'Snowball.'

'I am not calling her *Snowball*!' I say.

Back in the kitchen, Ronnie's standing on the little wooden step that Mr Thomas made him so he can reach the sink. He's elbow-deep in bubbles and singing 'Run Rabbit Run' really quietly.

Mrs Thomas is searching in her handbag; she looks up. 'Jimmy, be a love, would you? Nip to the shop and get us some bacon and oats, please. Here's the money.'

'Can't Ronnie go?' I ask.

'No,' Mrs Thomas says. 'I've asked you.'

'But …'

'No buts – just do as I ask.'

I've got no choice. I take the coins and turn sharply, my elbow catching a chair. It hits the floor with an echoing crash.

'Jimmy! Be careful,' Mrs Thomas says, her face and shoulders scrunched up tight.

'It was an accident.'

'Yes, bach, I know, but if you wake your Uncle Alun …'

'He's not my uncle!' And I don't know why I do it – something inside me just snaps – but as I pass the chair, I give it a good kick.

It's like time freezes. Florence gasps. Ronnie stops singing. I feel my cheeks burn but it's too late now.

Mrs Thomas glares at me before slowly picking up the chair and sliding it under the table. Her voice is an angry whisper, which is worse than being shouted at. 'Uncle or not, *Alun* needs his rest. He needs it because he goes down a filthy pit, digging and scraping for coal to keep this roof over our heads – *all* our heads, whether you like it or not. Now get to the shop.'

'It's all right, Aunty Gwen.' Ronnie's standing on

the floor, suds dripping off the ends of his fingers. 'I can go for you.'

Mrs Thomas answers him but keeps looking at me, her voice tight, like she's holding something in. 'No thank you, Ronnie. I've asked your brother.'

She pushes past. It sounds like she's gone into the parlour. I think I hear a sob. My face feels so hot; I never meant to make her cry.

Florence gives a low whistle. 'I bet she'd have slammed that door if Alun wasn't in bed.'

I shove the money deep into my pocket. 'Shut up, Florence.'

Ronnie sniffs. She goes over to him. 'Come on,' she says, helping him back on to the step. 'Clean those dishes up all nice, make your Aunty Gwen happy, eh?'

He nods and scrubs at the porridge bowls again. There's no singing now. Florence ducks into the pantry, comes out with a mop and bucket and starts wiping the soapy water off the floor.

'What are you doing?' I ask.

'Stopping you from getting a beating, that's what. If

we can get this place all neat and tidy, then they might not whack you.'

Ronnie's stopped again. He turns on the step and wobbles. He looks like he's just seen Hitler march through the kitchen. 'Florence! Uncle Alun and Aunty Gwen don't beat us.'

She looks at me.

'They don't,' I say.

'But she was properly angry,' Florence says. Her words sound a bit like a question.

'She wouldn't beat us though,' Ronnie says. 'Does Phyllis—'

'No,' Florence says quietly. 'Phyllis doesn't.'

She keeps looking towards the door, like she wants to run away.

'Just do the dishes, Ronnie,' I say, grabbing her by the arm and leading her out of the kitchen. 'We'll go to the shop.'

CHAPTER EIGHTEEN

FUGITIVES

We walk in silence. Every now and then Florence looks sideways at me but I keep my eyes ahead. We round the corner into Phyllis's street. There's a little gang just outside the shop, looks like lads. Four of them; one skinny and small, two huge and one normal-sized.

Florence spots them too. 'Blimey, I think it's—'

But she doesn't get to finish her sentence because scrawny Jack yells, 'Over there! Look! It's them!'

And suddenly three of the lads are running at us

full pelt. The other one – the normal-sized one – follows. I recognise his jumper; it's Duff.

For a split second, Florence looks like she wants to stand and fight, but even she isn't that tough. We turn and run, back along the street, down the hill. We race on, past all the side streets that look the same, down to the bottom where terraced houses flash past on our left. Angry shouts come from behind.

'Run, you filthy vaccies!'

'We'll smash you when we catch you!'

'We'll rip your stinking heads off!'

That was one of the twins. I reckon he *could* tear my head clean off if he wanted. And this is their turf. Even if we outrun them, we can't hide.

Just after the last house in the terrace, Florence makes a sharp left. 'Come on!' she screams. I look back; Jack's fallen over and they've all stopped to help him up. I sprint round the corner after her and see …

A dead end.

I bend over, gasping for breath. Thudding boots and shouts get louder. This is it. I'm going to die. I'm going to die in Wales with Florence flipping Campbell and I'll never see London again.

'Come on,' she whispers.

'Come on where?' I say. 'There *isn't* anywhere.'

We're standing on a small patch of concrete facing a shed. It's wedged between the last terraced house on the left and the huge, high wall of the Miners Institute on the right.

'There is.' She points to a narrow gap between the house and the shed.

'We'll never fit through there!' I don't want to try. I hate tight spaces.

She moves forward, presses her back against the wall and looks me up and down. 'Of course we will. There's space behind. I found it the other day, and you – you're not fat or anything. Just breathe in.'

She starts to move sideways like a crab, her head turned away from me. She reaches the back of the shed and disappears. From the road, the thud of boots gets even louder. My heart thumps hard against my ribs. The gap's so small.

But it's better than getting my head kicked in.

I edge my left shoulder in first, turning my face to the road so I can see them when they come. Taking a big breath, I squeeze in and shuffle along. My clothes scratch against the walls and it feels like my ears will tear off. I need to breathe out, there's too much air inside me. I keep moving but it feels like forever.

Oh heck, I'm stuck.

Thudding boots.

Closer.

I can't breathe. My head's fuzzy and light, like when I had the fever.

Boys run past, down the hill, sounding confused now.

'Where are they?'

That's Jack.

'They can't just disappear!'

That's Duff.

'You go that way, we'll look by the river.'

That's one of the twins.

I push.

I'm through.

I close my eyes and whisper, 'Thank you, God.'

We're in a tiny square, like the world's smallest schoolyard. To my left is the house; the institute's on the right and the shed is behind me now. In front is another wall, about five feet high, with railings running all along the top. Florence is leaning against it, her arms folded. 'You took your time.'

I rub my sore ears. I take my hands away and there's a bit of blood. Florence looks from my fingers to my face.

'Your ears are pretty big, eh?'

'They aren't.'

She cocks her head from side to side and I cover my ears, pretending to rub them again.

'Well …' she says, 'they're a bit sticky-outy.'

'That gap is tiny.'

'Not *that* tiny, my ears are fine.' She tucks some hair behind one and fiddles with her ribbon again.

'Perhaps I just have a bigger head than you,' I say, wiping the blood on my shorts.

She raises her eyebrows.

'You know what I mean,' I say.

Florence grins.

I push the toe of my shoe along the ground. A layer of black dirt crumples up, showing concrete underneath. There's nothing else around except a few old sweet wrappers and twigs.

'The lads all ran past,' I say. 'I saw them.'

'Good.'

'So what do we do now?'

Florence goes all dramatic. 'Lie low, Private Travers. The enemy is near.'

It makes me laugh. She moves her eyes about like she's watching for snipers. I try to speak but she holds a hand up to my face and makes her voice go deep and manly. 'Careful, Private – careless talk costs lives.'

Still laughing, I push her hand away. 'So we just wait here?'

'Got no choice, have we?' She sits down against the wall. 'Best to wait till the coast is clear.'

'How will we know?'

Florence shrugs. 'Dunno, but we're safer here and those two big lads can't even get through.'

'True.' I look at the gap and wonder how I did. 'Jack

could though, he's properly skinny.'

'Well, that wouldn't matter.' She holds her arm up and flexes her muscles like a circus strongman. 'We already know I can take him.'

CHAPTER NINETEEN

SECRETS

I walk around and around, running my fingers along the walls. Florence sits with her knees bent, scratching in the damp dirt with a stick.

'Do you think this is coal dust?' I say, scraping at the black ground with my shoe again.

'Must be,' she mutters. 'It gets everywhere, Phyllis says.'

I grab the stick.

'Hey!' Florence swipes at me but I hold it out of her reach.

'Noughts and crosses?' I say, sitting down and making a grid in the coal dust.

We play best of nine. A few times, Florence tries to take an extra go but I spot it. In the end I win five games to three. She's fuming.

'Best of eleven,' she says, grabbing the stick. She's quick at arithmetic. I have to think about it to make sure she isn't trying to cheat again.

'No, I've had enough now,' I say.

She huffs. 'Just because you won.'

'Of course.' I try grinning at her but she's obviously a bad loser.

Florence starts scratching the ground again. I sit down against the opposite wall.

'How did you know this was here?' I ask.

She doesn't look up. 'I did a recce. It pays to know your surroundings, especially in times of war.'

Florence has an odd way of speaking sometimes. I didn't notice in London because I never really talked to her.

'Hitler doesn't care about places like this,' I say.

'He might. Anyway, it wasn't Hitler we just had

to run from, was it? Hiding places are always handy.'

Florence scratches a picture into the coal dust.

I wonder why she needs places to hide but I don't know how to ask. So I just say it. 'Why did you think Mr and Mrs Thomas would beat me?'

Florence's stick stops, hovering over her picture. Her face all dark and scrunched up, she scribbles and scribbles hard into the dirt until her picture has gone. When she looks up at me, there are tears in her eyes. Angry ones, I reckon.

'Don't you ever get a thump?' she asks, quieter than I've ever heard her speak.

I look at the ground so I don't have to see her face. 'My nan slapped my legs when I was small, if I got too near the fire.'

'That's not what I mean. Those sorts of taps are nothing.' She throws the stick hard at the shed wall. It pings off and I have to dodge.

'Watch it, Florence!'

We sit there saying nothing for about a million years.

Florence gets up and paces around, looking at the sky, the walls, anywhere but at me.

'It's Mum mostly, that hits us. Me and my brothers and sisters.' She kicks at a dry patch of coal dust and a little cloud puffs up. 'Dad sometimes gives us a clout but we can usually get out of his way quick enough. But her ... she knows how to corner you.'

'Don't your brothers and sisters look out for you?'

'Them? The four oldest have left home now, got out as soon as they could. Can't blame them. The other three are just glad when they aren't the ones getting hit. If it's me then it's not them, is it?'

I feel sick. I could never let Ronnie take a beating for me. 'But you're the youngest! They're supposed to look after you.'

Her laugh comes out harsh. 'We're *Campbells*, Jimmy. We don't look after each other. We're not like you and Ronnie.'

I think back to all the times in PT when Florence got changed at the back of the classroom, of the bruises I saw on her arms and legs. Miss Goodhew asked her about them once and Florence said she bumped into things and fell over a lot. I don't think Miss Goodhew believed her. But she didn't do anything to help her either.

Florence sits down again, but next to me this time. Her voice is really small.

'You won't tell, will you?'

'I won't tell.'

'Cross your heart?'

'Cross my heart.' I make an X over my chest with my fingers.

I don't know if it's because she's trusted me with her secret or if I just want to change the subject again, but the words tumble out.

'I found a skull. In a tree. It's a human skull and I don't know how it got there or whose it is but it's real and I've got no flaming idea what to do about it!'

Her mouth hangs open, properly actually open, then she says, 'Scary.'

'Yeah.'

She whistles long and low, just like a boy.

'Bleurgh.' She shakes her shoulders, all dramatic

again. 'Horrible.' She thinks for a minute. 'So where's this tree?'

'Up the mountain.'

'And it was just a skull? No other bones?'

'I don't know.'

'What? Didn't you have a proper look?'

'I dropped it and ran like mad the first time,' I say. 'Then I went back and … I don't know … it wasn't so bad but then Ronnie came and—'

'Ronnie saw it! Is he all right?'

'He's fine now but it's why he wet himself the other day.'

'Oh,' she says. 'Poor Ronnie.'

An excited look comes over her face, like when she thought she was going to see a fox cub. 'Show me.' She's on her feet, pulling at me.

'All right! All right! Don't drag my blooming arm off!'

'And it's not a trick? You won't just get halfway there and leg it?' She gives me that hard stare again. 'Because you know I'll catch you.'

I stare back. 'I wouldn't do that.'

Florence grins and her nose wrinkles, it's

got freckles on. I've never noticed them before, perhaps on account of them being under all that dirt.

She moves towards the gap and a cold wave runs right through me. 'Florence, I … I don't think I can.' I scrape the coal dust with my heel. 'I don't like tight spaces.'

I wait for her to laugh at me but she just points to the wall with the railings on top. 'There's a playing field up there. That way might be better.'

I walk over to the wall to judge its height. 'I could give you a bunk-up.'

'All right.'

I make a cradle with my fingers for her foot. I hardly need to push; she weighs almost nothing. She pulls herself up easily and hangs from the railings with one hand and offers the other to me, and I suddenly get this feeling, like I know telling her was the right thing to do.

I grab her hand, grind one foot into a gap in the bricks and brace myself.

On the count of three, I push off the ground and

Florence pulls. I reach for the railings and seize hold. It's easy after that; we pull ourselves up and over the top.

'Up the mountain then?' I say.

'Yes! Onwards, Private Travers!' Florence calls, already running across the playing field. 'Operation Bones under way.'

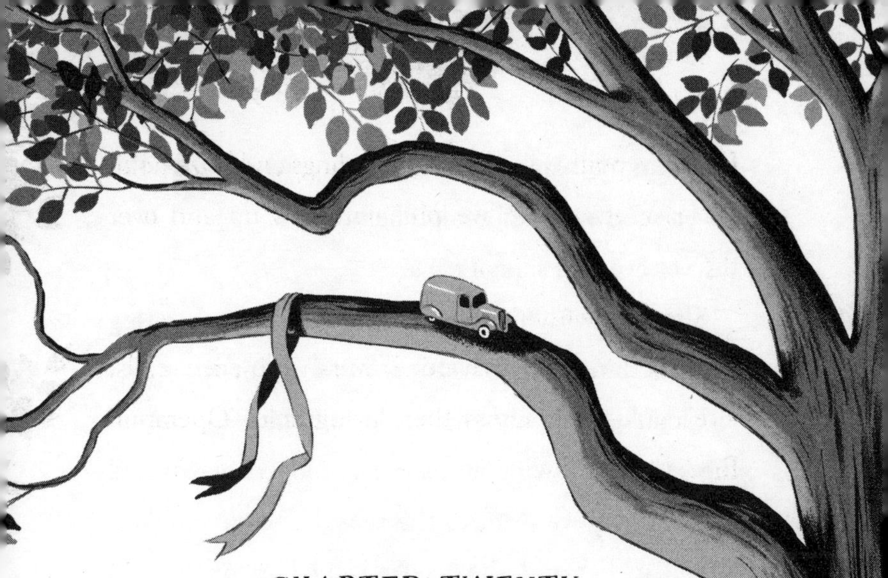

CHAPTER TWENTY

BONES

I follow her across the playing field and on to the Bryn, always looking for any sign of Jack and his gang, then it's up, up, up. Florence is a lot faster than me; she can really shift. She waits at a corner, then we run along the street to the fence that leads to the sloping fields. We race up the mountain, stopping at the stream for a minute, catching our breath.

'I love being so high,' she says, looking out over the valley. 'I've never seen anywhere as lovely as this.' I try to see what she sees but it's just great green lumps with bits of black from the mine. 'Mind you, I've never been outside London before now.'

'Not even on school trips?'

She narrows her eyes like she's really concentrating on something in the distance. 'Never went on one.'

I could kick myself. She'd watched us out of the classroom window as we'd trooped across the yard the day we went to the seaside. Some children waved to her and she'd poked out her tongue and made a rude sign with her fingers. When we were all talking about how much fun it was she said it was a stupid place and she hadn't wanted to go anyway.

'Come on,' I say. 'This is more exciting than any old school trip.'

We run again, up and up, me pointing out the way. The gate to the field is in the distance and I shout for her to stop there. When I catch up she's sitting on the top like it's a horse.

'Howdy, pardner.' She winks.

'You'd make a good cowgirl,' I say, leaning on the gate.

'I'd be brilliant at riding around and shooting mangy varmints – like in the Westerns.'

'How have you—' I stop myself.

'What? How have I seen a Western?' She leans close to my face. I can see her freckles again. 'I have been to the pictures, you know.'

'Oh.'

'Sneak in, don't I?' She swings her leg around and hops off the gate. 'Coming then, pardner?'

She won't hold it. Won't even come near it. I never thought Florence would be this afraid of the skull.

'It's just bone,' I say, sitting next to her on the grass. 'It can't hurt you.'

She moves backwards along the ground, not looking like a cocky cowgirl any more. '*You* ran away when you found it.'

I hold out the skull.

'No!' She jumps a bit. 'Don't be an idiot!'

'I wasn't trying to … Look … you wanted to see it and here it is.'

'Well, I've seen it now, so –' she waves her

hand like a princess waving away a peasant – 'put it back.'

I don't.

Florence looks at the hollow, then stands and walks all around the trunk.

'What are you doing?' I ask.

She kneels back down next to me. 'I reckon you could fit in there.'

'Florence, that gap you took me through next to the institute was bad enough – and I could still see the sky. I am *not* getting inside a flipping tree!' The hollow is so small and dark, it'll press on me and I'll freeze and be stuck in there with who knows what. 'You do it. You're smaller than me.'

She looks horrified. '*I'm* not doing it, there could be a hundred skulls in there!'

'Don't be daft.' But oh heck, there could be. What if it's the place a murderer kept all their victims' skulls?

'Go on then.'

I don't move.

'Oh, for pity's sake!' She pushes me roughly out of

the way. 'One of us needs to flaming well do it or we'll never find out what happened.'

I watch Florence crawl into the hollow. I stare at the soles of her new shoes.

Half a minute later she shuffles backwards so fast she almost kicks me.

'Bones,' she whispers. 'Lots of them. But no more skulls.' She sits up, redoing her ribbon. 'I think it's just one person, but if you make me go in there again I swear I'll clock you one.'

'Fair enough.' I smile. 'Thanks for looking.'

She smiles back. 'Where do you think they came from?'

'I haven't worked that out yet—'

'Ooooh,' she says, 'I know!'

I raise my eyebrows.

'It's probably a miner, there are loads of them round here. I bet he got drunk in the pub, got into a fight and was … murdered.' She looks very pleased with herself. When I say nothing, she carries on. 'All right then, how about a Victorian poacher? Shot – murdered – for nicking pheasants.'

'This isn't a game,' I say.

'A German spy!'

'Also murdered, I suppose?'

She pulls a face. 'All right then, smarty-pants – *you* tell me who it is.'

'I don't know, do I? Maybe there's no murderer.'

'Jimmy, people don't just go and die inside trees. And there's a dent and a crack in the skull. *Something* bad must have happened.'

'All I know is you aren't helping.' I run my fingers over the top of the skull. 'But I think they must have been there for years, and maybe they weren't just bones when they … when they went inside the hollow. I think someone put a whole dead body in and the bones got separated somehow.'

Florence fiddles with her ribbon. 'Animals?'

'I suppose.'

We sit in silence, me leaning on the tree trunk and her a few feet away on the grass. After a few minutes, Florence shuffles towards me. She turns away and holds her hand out. 'Go on then, pass it here. The skull. Pass it here.'

Suddenly I don't want to give it to her.

'What's the matter?' she asks, facing me properly now.

'Two hands,' I say. 'And you have to hold it really carefully.'

She nods and I place the skull in her open palms. Her fingers close around it and she breathes out slowly. She tilts the skull towards her.

'Urgh! Take it back!' She closes her eyes and holds her arms out straight. 'I can't … Quick! Just take it!'

I snatch it off her, holding it tightly. 'Let's go, we need to see what we can find out. Starting with how long it takes a person to become bones. But you can't tell anyone. We don't know who we can trust.'

'Of course. Loose lips sink ships.' She grins. 'I'll see if there's anything in Ieuan's nature books. He won't know what I'm up to.'

'All right. But be careful.'

I put the skull back.

She looks at the hollow. 'If this is so secret, we

should cover the gap with branches, so the likes of Jack Evans can't find it.'

'Good idea.'

'That's me,' she says, tapping her head with her finger. 'The brains of this operation.'

CHAPTER TWENTY-ONE

HALF A SANDWICH

Halfway down the mountain I remember the shopping. Mrs Thomas is already cross with me; now she'll think I did it on purpose and I'll be in even more trouble. Florence goes straight through to the back of the shop to 'write down clues' and I join the queue behind three women who chat and fuss like the chickens. I rub the stitch in my side and wait for my turn but the last one just wants to talk and talk.

'Come on,' I mutter. She turns around and frowns at me. Welsh women must have the hearing of a flipping bat. I know her; she's the one who was scrubbing her step, the purple-hat woman from the institute. 'Sorry.' I try to win her over with a smile. It doesn't work. I'm not Ronnie. 'It's just that I'm in a hurry.'

She looks me right up and down like she's never seen a boy before. 'And what if *I'm* in a hurry? You haven't thought about that, have you? No!' She looks closer. 'Oh, it's *you*.'

The way she was gossiping, she didn't look like she was in a hurry. But I'd better not say so. She turns back to Phyllis.

'Here we are sending off good boys like my John to fight Hitler, and look what Llanbryn gets in return! Thieves and vagabonds! Mind you –' she jerks her head towards me and makes her voice a pretend whisper – 'some have found a place where they can fit right in, haven't they?'

'I haven't stolen anything!' I say, feeling the blood pound in my head.

'Well, nothing started going missing till you lot came here.'

'So no flaming Welsh person has ever been a thief?'

The woman turns, all puffed up like a prize hen. 'Just who do you think you're speaking to? If I thought it would do any good, I'd have a word with Gwen Thomas, but—'

'That's enough!' Phyllis's voice blasts through the air like a gunshot. She takes a big breath and blows it out slowly. 'Mrs Ringrose, I'd appreciate you keeping your narrow-minded comments to yourself while in my establishment. And, Jimmy, keep a lid on it, bach, you're doing yourself no favours!'

Mrs Ringrose glares at us both before huffing out of the shop. I get the shopping and rush back to Heol Mabon thinking – again – that some people around here don't like the Thomases at all.

Mr Thomas is in the living room reading the paper. He looks over the top of it when I burst in. On the arm of his chair is a plate with crumbs and smears of dripping. I just stand still, opening and closing my mouth like a stupid fish.

He nods once. 'Jimmy.'

That's all he says.

I mumble hello and stare really hard at the rug till

the flower pattern blurs. Mr Thomas looks at the shopping in my hand. 'You'd better go and put those away in the pantry before Gwen gets back.'

'Where is she?' I ask.

'Gone to see her cousin Jean in Aberbeeg. Took your brother on the bus and left me a note for when I got up. Said you'd gone to Phyllis's.'

'He'll love that,' I say quietly. 'The bus, I mean.'

'He will.'

Then it all rushes out of my mouth like a balloon deflating. 'Florence and me went straight to the shop, honest we did, but some boys chased us and we had to hide. Then we …' What do I say? I can't tell him about the tree. 'I'm sorry about your breakfast.'

'Doesn't matter.'

'This is your bacon,' I say like an idiot.

He disappears behind the newspaper again. 'Know how to fry it?'

'Yes.'

'Off you go then. Bread and dripping's nice but it's not bacon.'

I go into the kitchen and take the pan down from

its hook on the wall. While the bacon fries I cut some bread. Mrs Thomas's note is on the kitchen table; it says just what Mr Thomas said it did. Nothing about me upsetting her. I suppose that'll come later – she probably wants to tell him face to face – and he'll think I'm awful and, I don't know why, but that bothers me. I make the sandwich really nice.

When I take it to him, Mr Thomas has put down the paper and is rubbing his eyes.

'The bread's a bit wonky,' I say. 'Sorry.'

He takes a bite. 'How's it so crispy?' He presses it between his fingers.

'I fried it in the bacon fat at the end. My dad likes it that way.'

'Does he now?' He puts it down.

Oh heck, he hates it. I've ruined his sandwich.

But then he smiles.

'Your dad might be on to something,' he says. 'Now what's this about boys chasing you and Flossie?'

I shove my hands deep in my pockets. 'Oh, it's nothing. We can look after ourselves.'

'Not the ones who picked on Ronnie, were they?

The vicar's boy and your London mate?'

'He's not my mate,' I say. 'Not any more.'

'So it was, then.'

'Yeah.'

'You watch that Jack Evans. Nasty sort, he is.' Mr Thomas picks up his sandwich again. 'Thanks for the grub.' He glances towards the kitchen. 'Where's yours?'

'I'm not hungry.'

'Nonsense. Boys are always hungry. Here, have this.' Mr Thomas lifts the other half of his sandwich and offers it to me. I don't move.

'No need to be proud with me, bach. Here.'

I take it.

'Better get a plate,' Mr Thomas says. 'Or you'll be for it when Gwen gets back.'

I feel like sitting down with Mr Thomas so we can eat together but it's probably just the sandwich making me miss Dad. And he's not Dad so I get a plate and sit at the kitchen table.

In the bedroom, I put down my *Hotspur* comic and pick up a little flip book. Ronnie and Mr Thomas made it after the party. They spent ages at the kitchen table cutting paper and drawing and colouring. When they'd finished, Mrs Thomas sewed it all together and said Ronnie was a proper author.

Now I lie back on my pillow, flip flip flipping really fast to watch the yellow Dinky van drive across the pages.

Flip flip flip …

Flip flip flip …

Till my eyes go blurry and I'm not even seeing the drawing any more, or thinking much at all, and the tree and the bones come into my head. Again. How could a whole person even fit in there? They'd have to be small.

The front door bangs.

'No running in the house!' Mrs Thomas calls after Ronnie as he thunders down the passage. Their voices get muffled when they reach the living room. I pick at the candlewick on the bedspread, just like I told Ronnie not to do.

'Jiiiiiimmy!' Ronnie's racing up the stairs. 'Jimmy! I went on a bus!'

He bursts into the bedroom, beaming and panting. I sit up. 'Was it good?'

'It was brilliant! We went all over Wales and most of it's green, except for the pits and the coal heaps, and we went up a hill so big I thought we'd roll back down but we didn't. And the bus driver said a bad swear and Aunty Gwen told him off and I met our new aunty, Aunty Jean, and she gave me this.' He shoves a small paper bag into my hand and grins up at me.

'You've been *all over* Wales?' I say.

He nods. I open the bag. Fudge.

'Aunty Jean made it,' Ronnie says, taking a big piece.

'Not everyone in Wales is your aunty, you know.'

'I know. Just Aunty Gwen and Aunty Jean.' He looks so flipping pleased about it.

'Don't speak with your mouth full.'

He swallows. 'Where's Florence?'

'At home.' That word. It's true, I suppose. It's more of a home than she's got in London.

'I'll save her some fudge,' he says, taking the bag and scrunching up the top.

'She lives in a *shop*, Ronnie. With sweets.'

'I'm still saving her some. She's my friend.'

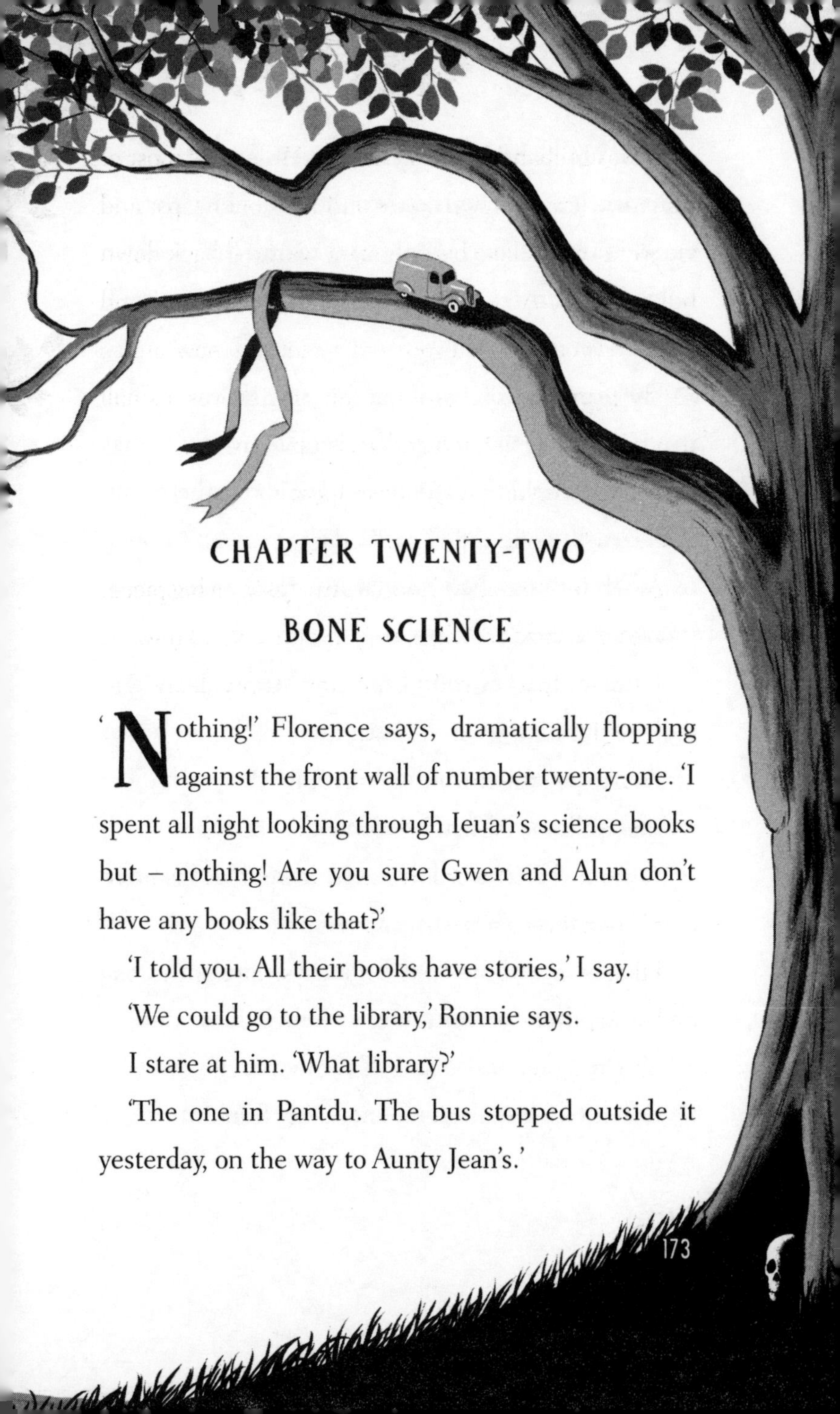

CHAPTER TWENTY-TWO

BONE SCIENCE

'Nothing!' Florence says, dramatically flopping against the front wall of number twenty-one. 'I spent all night looking through Ieuan's science books but – nothing! Are you sure Gwen and Alun don't have any books like that?'

'I told you. All their books have stories,' I say.

'We could go to the library,' Ronnie says.

I stare at him. 'What library?'

'The one in Pantdu. The bus stopped outside it yesterday, on the way to Aunty Jean's.'

'Pantdu's the next village,' Florence says. 'I saw signs for it from the train on the way here. Bet we could walk it. There's only one main road, we can follow it and there'll be signs. And if we get lost we'll just ask someone.'

The road out of Llanbryn follows the river along the bottom of the valley. We set off. Mrs Thomas didn't say anything about yesterday, about the bacon and oats. But she didn't really look at me all through tea so I went to bed early with my comics. Even though she didn't tell me to.

I pull my jacket round me. It's colder today and dark clouds fill the sky. I thought telling Ronnie about all the bones would trouble him more than it did. He looked a bit scared, but he didn't wet himself so that's something. He just said he was glad that Florence knows because she's the cleverest of all of us. I let him get away with that one because it's probably true. Florence offers round a bag of jelly babies. Ronnie takes a red one and bites off the head. She nibbles the other end of her green one. 'They can't run away if you start with the feet.'

Ronnie and me laugh.

The sky gets darker and the clouds get fatter. We speed up but, still, three buses have passed us by the time we get to the library.

The building is old and small. I hope they have enough science books or we've had a really long walk for nothing. And we still have to walk back.

We go up the steps and Florence pushes open the heavy doors. Behind the front desk, a man puts cards into a cabinet of little wooden drawers. He glances at us. 'Children's books to your right.'

'Actually, we don't want the children's books,' Florence says. She's using a voice I've never heard her use before. A trying-to-be-posh one. 'Please can you tell us where the science section is?'

The man puts down the cards. 'English, are you?'

'Yes,' she says.

'Evacuees, is it?'

Not this again.

She nods. 'If you can just tell us where the science section is, I can find what I need. It's for my homework and I won't get top marks if I get my facts from children's books.'

She's thought of everything.

The man smiles. 'That's what I like to see, an enquiring mind. You can't borrow books from the adult section without an adult ticket though.'

'I don't need to take them out. I just need to look something up.'

He smiles at her again. 'Aren't you a scholar? What type of science do you need?'

'Bone science,' Ronnie says, before we can stop him.

'Biology,' Florence says quickly. 'He means biology.'

'I'll show you,' the librarian says. We follow him through some more doors into the adult section; it's very quiet. A few grown-ups stare at us, as if we shouldn't be in their section at all.

Right at the far end, the man stops. 'The biology books are here. It's all labelled. If you can't find what you need, come and get me, but a clever girl like you shouldn't have any trouble.' He turns to Ronnie and me. 'And make sure you whisper.'

He's right. She doesn't have any trouble; Florence soon finds the right chapter in a book called *Human Anatomy*.

'How did you do that?' I ask.

'Do what?' Florence whispers.

'Find it so quickly.'

'I go in the Fieldway library all the time back home. It's nice and warm and quiet.'

She means it's the opposite of her house, and I wonder again at how much I didn't know about her before we came here.

'Look.' Florence points to a page with a drawing of a skeleton. 'It says here two hundred and six – that's how many bones there should be. Good to know, but not what we need right now.'

'Blimey, that's a lot,' I say, forgetting to whisper.

A man in the military section tuts loudly. I stare at the diagram and think of the bones, think of the person in the tree.

Florence flicks through a few more pages. 'Ah, here we go – decomposition.'

Ronnie peers at the pictures and winces. I find a

book on animals and give it to him. Florence runs her finger down the paragraphs, turns over and keeps going. At the end of the next page she stops. 'It says here between eight and twelve years for a human body to decompose – longer if it's well buried.' She looks up. 'That's about as long as we've been alive.'

'Rules out a murderer hanging around,' I say. 'Surely they'd have killed again by now.'

'Can we go?' Ronnie asks. 'Florence's book is horrible.'

She closes it. 'So what's our next move, Private Travers?'

'We'll go up to the tree tomorrow. Have a closer look.' I take Ronnie's hand and try not to think about going inside the hollow. 'Come on then.'

We make our way quietly through the adult section, say goodbye to the librarian and push open the heavy doors into the pouring rain. It's going to be a long, wet walk back to Llanbryn.

CHAPTER TWENTY-THREE

DARK DAYS

Mr and Mrs Thomas are in the living room. She's crying.

I hate it when grown-ups cry. It's like the world is the wrong way up. After Mum left, I sometimes heard Dad crying in their bedroom. One night there was a crash against the wall and the next day one of Mum's favourite vases was in the bin. That's when he swapped rooms with us.

Ronnie and me are in the garden. He's talking to the chickens but I don't suppose they care very much about his Dinky van or the letter we got from Nan this morning. People keep saying there'll be no bombs in the Valleys; they sent us here to keep us safe. The war won't happen in Llanbryn, they say.

Except, in a way, it already has.

Mrs Ringrose's son, John, has been killed near his army training camp. Car crash. He didn't even get to the war. His mother got a telegram and it's his funeral today. His father works down the pit with Mr Thomas and everyone is really sad and keeps saying these are 'dark days'.

But I don't think that's what's making Mrs Thomas cry. She took some eggs to Mrs Ringrose but Mrs Ringrose didn't want them. Mr Thomas said he didn't know why she'd bothered. I thought they were going to argue, like Mum and Dad used to, but she started to cry and Mr Thomas is sitting with her now.

'Let's go and call for Florence,' I say. 'We need to go to the tree.'

'All right,' Ronnie says, waving goodbye to Dorothy and the others through the chicken wire.

Inside, he launches himself like a little space rocket. He flings his arms around Mrs Thomas and almost pushes Mr Thomas off the chair. She laughs and holds him really tight, kissing the top of his head. 'Ronnie Travers, I have to say, for an English boy you give a good Welsh cwtch.'

When we step on to the pavement, Ronnie's face crumples like Mrs Thomas's hanky.

'Flipping heck, what're *you* crying for?' I say.

'I don't want Aunty Gwen to be sad.' He sniffs and raises his arm to his face.

'Wipe your nose on your sleeve and she'll be more than sad,' I say. 'She'll be flaming furious.'

It's all black. The cars and the people's clothes make a dark river that flows up through Llanbryn instead of down. From a spot on the mountain, Ronnie, Florence and me sit closer together than we need to and watch the funeral procession. It winds its way up from the dead soldier Ringrose's house along the streets to the church. People are standing on their doorsteps, hats off, heads bowed. Then, as the last car passes, they join the end and become part of it. Mrs Thomas walks with Phyllis, their arms looped together. Mr Thomas refused to go.

'I'm not going,' he'd said this morning. 'And that's an end to it.'

'I know it's hard for you, Alun,' Mrs Thomas said. 'But think how it looks.'

'I don't care how it looks. The gossips round here will feast on Alun Thomas no matter what. One more story won't make a difference.'

She asked Ronnie and me to leave the kitchen then, but we stayed on the stairs to listen.

'But he was a soldier, Alun. And he hadn't even got as far as fighting … It's …'

'Cruel? Unfair? That's life. I know that better than most. And I don't see why you're going. That Ringrose woman has been nothing but horrible to you since …'

'Since I became a Thomas?'

Silence.

She carries on. 'You know I've never cared about that and I've never cared about Hilda Ringrose, but

John was a nice boy. Despite his mother. He was always polite and pleasant to us.' Mrs Thomas sniffed. 'What about me?' Her voice went quieter. 'Don't I matter?'

A chair scuffed the kitchen floor. I think he must have gone over to her. 'You're all that matters.' Mr Thomas didn't sound cross any more. 'But I can't go. You know why, Gwen. It's about more than Hilda Ringrose.'

'I know.'

Footsteps. The back door opened and closed. We went upstairs and Ronnie drove his Dinky van over the bedspread, up and down the fluffy candlewick.

Now, Mr Ringrose helps Mrs Ringrose out of the second car. Jack Evans's dad, dressed in full vicar robes, steps forward to shake their hands. The river of black forms a puddle around the church gates and six men lift Private John Ringrose's coffin out of the back of the hearse.

It takes ages for everyone to follow it into the church.

'What happens in a funeral?' Ronnie asks.

'The vicar says nice things about the dead person and people cry and sing hymns,' Florence says, picking a daisy and spinning its stem in her fingers.

'What about the coffin?'

'That gets buried in the ground.'

'In a grave?'

She nods.

Ronnie picks a daisy too. 'I'm going to make you a necklace,' he says. 'I'm good at daisy chains, aren't I, Jimmy?'

I smile. 'For someone with fat little sausage fingers, you do a decent job.'

He pokes his tongue out at me and turns to Florence. 'Our mum showed me.'

The smile slips off my face like melted butter.

'What happened to her?' Florence asks.

Ronnie puts his head down and concentrates really hard on piercing the daisy stem with his fingernail.

'She ran off with the butcher from Green Lane,' I say. 'Some people say they're in Ramsgate, some say Southend. Don't know why they would go there, she hates the seaside.'

Ronnie's tongue is sticking out and he's frowning hard as he threads a stem through the hole he made.

'I heard rumours,' Florence says. 'Do you miss her?'

'Sometimes. Not really. I don't know.' I shrug. 'It's Nan and Dad who always looked after us.' I nod at Ronnie and mouth, 'He does though.'

Florence ruffles Ronnie's hair. 'How are you getting on?' He holds up a chain of three squashed daisies. 'Well, that's just beautiful,' she says.

They're lowering the coffin into the ground. Mr and Mrs Ringrose hold each other up. Jack Evans's dad is saying words we can't hear. People throw handfuls of dark, Welsh dirt into the grave. Some throw flowers. Once they've all gone, two men come with shovels and scoop piles of earth on top of Private John Ringrose.

That's it.

The first funeral I've ever seen.

Florence sighs. 'Up to the tree then, troops?'

I shake my head. 'I've had enough of death for one day.'

CHAPTER TWENTY-FOUR

THE SEARCH PARTY

Dad's sent us a picture postcard of Tower Bridge. He says he'll take us there when the war is over and we can have a picnic and watch the ships go past. Sitting here on the garden bench, I imagine Dad, Nan, Ronnie and me eating sandwiches and cake right next to the Thames. I want to be there now.

There's a thud and Mrs Thomas comes flying out of the back door. 'I can't find Ronnie! He's not out here, is he?'

'No, I thought he was playing upstairs.'

Her eyes dart everywhere. 'So did I, but he isn't.'

'He's not out here, either,' I say, standing up. 'I'd have seen him.'

She looks in the air-raid shelter anyway.

Thoughts tap at my head like a tiny hammer. Bones. A murderer.

It was more than ten years ago. Ronnie will be fine.

But the tapping doesn't stop.

Mrs Thomas rushes into the house, muttering about checking the wardrobes. I follow. 'He hid under the bed once,' I call. 'When he was being a pain.'

That must be it – he must be hiding – playing a game, that's all.

She thunders up the stairs. I hear her pull Ronnie's mattress across the floor, then shove it back again. I shout up from the passage. 'I'll look in the street.'

'Yes – do that!' It sounds like she's in their bedroom now. He won't be in there; even Ronnie wouldn't go in there.

I run up and down Heol Mabon, checking the hill at each end, but I can't see him. I shout but no one answers. I'm just running back to the house when

Mrs Maddock the tortoise opens the top window next door.

'What do you think you're doing bellowing in the street? Got a bell in every tooth, you have!'

'I'm looking for my brother.'

'Passed my front window about an hour ago.' She straightens the net curtain.

'Which way did he go?'

'Manners cost nothing, you know.'

'*Please*.'

'Now let me think …'

Mrs Maddock doesn't need to think. Mrs Maddock knows everything that happens in this street because she's always in the flaming window.

'That way.' She points towards the Bryn. If she thinks I'm going to thank her, she can whistle. When I get back in the house, Mrs Thomas is in the passage.

'Mrs Maddock saw him go out about an hour ago,' I say.

She tugs at the straps of her pinny. 'But he knows not to go without letting me know.'

I grab my jacket. 'I'll go and have a proper look

around, I know the places he likes. He's probably just gone to call for Florence.'

Please let that be true.

She manages a smile. 'All right. But straight back once you've found him, mind.'

Ieuan says Phyllis has taken Florence out for the morning and he hasn't seen Ronnie at all. I head up the mountain, jumping and twitching at every little sound. Flipping countryside. Everything's so quiet you could hear a mouse sneeze and think it's a bomb. There's no sign of him. The little hammer turns into a mallet as I walk towards the tree.

But the branches we put over the entrance haven't been disturbed. I'm sure of it. And I don't know why, but all the breath comes out of me in a strange sort of dry sob.

I'll go back; he's probably in the kitchen stuffing his face with bread and dripping by now. Just as I'm climbing over the gate, something – someone? – moves in the hedgerow. There's a rustling sound. I stand very still. 'Ronnie?'

A large black bird flies screeching into the air.

Flipping stupid countryside.

Mrs Thomas is getting more and more frantic. I put the kettle on for a cup of really strong, sweet tea. Nan says it's good for shock.

We sit at the table, not saying a word. The hammer tap-tap-taps inside my head. I can't tell her how worried I am. I wish Mr Thomas was here. He doesn't get in a tizzy. He'd know what to do and where to look.

'Honey!' Mrs Thomas's cup hits its saucer with a clatter, tea slopping over the side.

'Pardon?'

'Ronnie was asking if he could go and see Mrs Powell's beehives, that's where he'll be.'

Blimey, I hope she's right.

There's a noise from the passage and we both jump up and almost run to the front door. Mr Thomas is standing there black as the night. I've never seen him come straight from a shift before. His eyes and teeth are very white in his dark face.

'What's the matter?' he says, taking off his cap.

I wait for Mrs Thomas to say something but all that comes out of her mouth is a strangled squeak.

Mr Thomas tilts his head as if searching for something behind us. 'Where's Ronnie?' There's a tone in his voice, a look on his face that I can't work out. Just like how Mrs Thomas was in the garden.

'We don't know,' I say. 'He went out and hasn't come back.'

Mr Thomas twists his cap up tight in his big, dark hands. 'How long?'

'Nearly three hours now. I've been out but I couldn't find him.'

Mr Thomas shakes out his cap. Coal dust floats to the floor but Mrs Thomas doesn't even notice. He puts his cap back on. 'I'm going down to the institute to find Ceri Bevan. He can organise a search party. Jimmy, fetch Florence and get some doors knocked, someone must have seen your brother. Send any adults who want to help to the institute. Gwen, you need to stay here in case he turns up. I'll ask Ceri if Margaret can come and sit with you.'

Mrs Thomas nods through her tears.

The tapping in my head gets quieter. Mr Thomas sounds like a soldier planning a military operation. He sounds like Florence. We're bound to find Ronnie now. I follow him out on to the pavement and he grabs me by the shoulders. For one awful second I think he's going to tell me off for not looking after my little brother, but then he says, 'We'll find him, Jimmy.' Except the fear in his eyes tells me he's as worried as I am.

CHAPTER TWENTY-FIVE

A GOOD LOOK OVER THE VALLEY

'Why are your shoulders black?' Florence wrinkles her nose as we knock on the door next to Phyllis's shop.

'Mr Thomas took hold of me.' I see the shock on her face. 'No – not in a rough way. He's still dirty from work.'

'Didn't he have a wash?' she asks. 'I mean, he must have been really worried if he didn't even have a wash.'

'I don't know, do I?' I tap my foot on the pavement. *Answer the door, answer the door.* 'I'm going over there,'

I say, pointing across the road. 'It'll be quicker if we take one side each.'

'Good idea.'

We get knocking. Before long there are lots of people grabbing coats, saying they'll help. Some go to the institute like Mr Thomas asked; some tear off on their own. Some just say he's a daft little boy who'll come home when he's hungry. One says he probably ran away to London because he stole the church collection money. Florence has to pull me away from that doorstep.

By the middle of the afternoon word's got around. Most of the doors we knock are unanswered or we're told that someone in the house has already gone to look for Ronnie. Florence and me sit on the fence looking up to the mountain.

'Are you *sure* he wasn't at the tree?' she asks for the hundredth time.

'*Yes*,' I say. 'I did hear a noise in the hedgerow, but it was only a bird.'

'What?'

'A bird. You know, flappy thing with wings. Flew out of the hedge and into the sky.'

She pulls a face, then looks at me too hard and too long. 'Jimmy, there's no murderer round here, you know. If there was, he'd have killed more people by now.'

There's no point pretending I was thinking of anything else. 'I hope you're right.'

'I am,' she says. Then, 'Do you think someone in the hedge could have spooked that bird?'

'I suppose.'

'Wait here!' She runs like mad back down the street. There's no point asking what she's doing; she's already so far away she wouldn't hear me.

I rack my brain to think of anywhere else Ronnie might go. After only a few minutes, Florence is back with a brown leather case slung across her body. It bumps against her gas mask box.

'What's that?' I ask.

'You'll see.' She taps the side of her nose and winks.

Before I can tell her how annoying she is, she's over the fence and halfway up the field.

Florence says we need to be up in the tree so we can get a good look over the valley. We leave our gas mask boxes at the bottom and climb to the end of the thickest branch, where there aren't as many leaves. I see green fields, black coal tips, rows and rows of houses. But no Ronnie. *Where is he?*

Florence lifts the brown leather case and pulls out a pair of binoculars. I reach out but she snatches them away.

'*You* can't have them!'

'Crikey, Florence, it's not like I'm taking your flipping ribbon!'

'Very funny.' She pokes out her tongue. 'They're Ieuan's – for birdwatching. And he doesn't know I've got them. I don't think he'll mind when he knows why I took them though.'

Florence makes a big show of putting the strap around her neck and moving the wheel.

'Anything?' I ask.

'The gate looks so much closer; I can even see the latch we never use!'

'Never mind the blooming gate! Can you see Ronnie?'

'No, but there are some people by the stream. They're probably looking for him too.'

She turns to the next field, the one with the footpath that leads to the church. It looks like she's following it down the mountain. She stops still and twiddles the wheel.

'Jimmy.' Her voice is an excited whisper. 'There's something in the corner a couple of fields down.' She lowers the binoculars. 'Looks like a den.'

We stop running when we reach the footpath. A little way along, there's one of those gates that isn't a gate. Florence says it's called a stile. We stand on it and look across the field. She's right; it is a den, made of planks of wood and corrugated iron. Thick tarpaulin fixed to the ground with tent pegs makes a roof. There's a sign over the door: *The Bunker*.

A pair of hands moves the iron sheet away and one of the twins comes out. He snaps a stick off a tree and goes back in. Florence and me look at each other.

'Jack's gang,' I mutter. 'They wouldn't tell us if they'd seen Ronnie or not.'

'Let's keep looking then.'

We jump down, carry on along the footpath, then turn left around the field, keeping low and quiet because the den's on the other side of the hedge. Just as we reach the corner, there's a whimpering sound. It's coming from the Bunker. I grab Florence's arm and we freeze.

Someone speaks. 'He isn't going to tell us, Evs.'

A London accent.

It's Duff.

'Oh, he will,' comes Jack's sneering voice. 'All it takes is the right ... *persuasion*.'

Florence looks terrified. 'Jimmy, I think they're bullying someone in there.'

The next voice is small but bold.

'You can't make me, you stinking Welsh pig!'

The swish of a stick. A cry of pain. Someone just hurt my little brother.

CHAPTER TWENTY-SIX

THE BUNKER

I run so fast not even Florence can keep up with me. Back along the footpath, round the corner and over the stile so quickly my foot catches at the top and I land with a thud that knocks all the breath out of my lungs. I push myself upright, take two big painful gulps of air and run on. I can feel Florence speeding along behind me. The den rushes up to meet us.

I rip the corrugated iron away and the sign flies off on to the ground. Inside, in the gloomy dark, four pairs of shocked eyes stare back at me. Jack, Duff, Gareth and Aled take a second to realise what's happening. But then, so do I …

The shaft of light coming from the doorway shows Ronnie sitting on an upturned milk crate, shaking like a puppy in the rain. They've blindfolded him. It looks like they've torn a bit off an old shirt to do it. It's darker where his tears have soaked through. What kind of a person does this?

'Ronnie.' My voice isn't much more than a breath, and I can't believe it but he smiles.

'I knew you'd come, Jimmy! I knew it!'

'I'm here too,' says Florence, squeezing past me and gently lifting the blindfold. Her blue eyes are icy as she looks at the boys. 'You're twisted – the lot of you.'

She puts her arms around Ronnie and he cuddles into her, his breaths calming down.

Jack sneers. 'Vaccies to the rescue, eh?'

Florence stands straight and tall, making Jack look even weedier. 'Yeah, we stick together.'

I look at Duff. 'Some of us do.'

He stares back at me, his eyes filled with spite. He

turns to Florence. 'So what are *you* going to do? Stink us out?'

Jack and the twins laugh stupidly. I see the shame that flashes across Florence's face – but only for a split second.

'I'll tell you what I'm going to do.' She nudges Ronnie towards the doorway. 'I'll smash your weaselly little faces in, won't I?' She nods at Jack. 'I've done it before.'

She's actually pushing up her sleeves and I feel this fierce pride for her. But there are four of them and three of us; the twins add up to two each, and Ronnie barely counts. No matter how much I want to hurt Jack, to grind him into the floor of this den, I know we're outnumbered.

They'll hammer us.

We have to get out of here. Fast. I push Ronnie a bit closer to the doorway, hoping Florence can see that our only choice is to scarper.

'Need a girl to fight your battles for you, Jimmy?' Jack says.

I shake my head. 'Not *for* me, *with* me. And this isn't over.'

Florence grins.

'Oh, I'm so scared,' the twin with glasses – Gareth? – says in a baby voice.

I shove Ronnie outside and step out after him, knowing Florence is behind us. I turn to my brother. 'Ronnie, can you run?' He nods. 'Then get ready.'

'Ready for what?' he says, but before the last word is fully out of his mouth, I kick hard at the den's wall. One. Two. Florence joins in with the third, whooping and yelling. The Bunker collapses, dragging the tarpaulin with it.

Angry shouts and filthy swears burst out of Jack Evans's clubhouse as it all caves in on them.

'Run!' I shout, stamping hard on the sign for the Bunker. It splits in two. Good. We leg it across the fields and down the mountain. The path becomes a track, I'm practically dragging Ronnie's arm out of its socket and his legs are going like heck. Florence is out in front. She makes a sudden turn and drops out of sight. We follow to find she's dived into a ditch at the side of the track. I hurl Ronnie in on top of her. He lands with an '*Oooph*' and I jump in too.

'Good … thinking,' I say, panting for breath. 'We were … never going to … outrun them with Ro—'

'Shh!' Florence sticks one hand over my mouth and one over Ronnie's. None of us moves a muscle as Jack, Duff and the twins race past. We wait a few minutes before flopping back against the soft grass of the ditch.

'Ronnie, what happened?' I ask.

He bites his bottom lip.

'You can tell us,' Florence adds.

'Promise you won't get cross?' He runs his hand over the long grass.

Florence and me share a look that says *This won't be good* but make the *Cross my heart* sign over our chests.

It all rushes out of him. 'I went up to the tree – I know I shouldn't have gone on my own but, after the funeral, you didn't want to and I thought I could help.'

I feel Florence's eyes on me.

He carries on. 'But I couldn't make myself look in the hollow. Coming down, I saw you, and I hid in a hedge because I thought you'd tell me off.'

'I knew it!' Florence says.

'Then I saw Jack and those boys and they wanted to know where I'd been. I wouldn't tell them so they said they'd have to put me under military arrest as a traitor and they made me go with them to their clubhouse.'

'Gits,' Florence says.

I nod for him to carry on.

'They … they said –' his voice cracks, and tears come to his big eyes – 'I wasn't from London at all. They said I was more likely a German spy and I had to tell them everything or they'd hurt me.'

Anger bubbles and boils inside me. Ronnie keeps talking. 'Jack hit me with a stick.' He holds out his arms; they're swollen with striped red marks. 'Then it broke so they had to get another one.'

'I'm going to kill Jack Evans,' I mutter.

'Not if I kill him first,' Florence says.

'And I didn't mean to, Jimmy, I swear I didn't but …'

'Go on,' I say slowly, worried about what might come next.

'They were being so horrible it just came out. I said I would never tell where … where the skull is, and he said, "What skull?" I didn't say another word, Jimmy. Honest.'

Silence. Florence and me glance at each other.

'You promised you wouldn't be cross,' Ronnie whispers.

And I realise I'm not.

'Come here.' I pull him towards me. 'You know what? We heard you. We heard you stick up for yourself.' He wriggles away slightly and looks up at me. 'So I'm not cross with you, I'm proud. All right, so something slipped out, but most people – bigger, older boys than you – would have told them everything.'

I kiss the top of his head. I don't even care that Florence is watching.

We tear along the top streets of Llanbryn, turn right, and slam straight into a group of men on the corner. One of them is Mr Thomas. He sees it's us and all the air rushes out of him in an odd, broken way. He crouches down in front of Ronnie. 'Where've you been, boy? Oh! Look at your arms!'

'Jack Evans and his gang,' Florence says. 'They kidnapped him.'

'What?' Mr Thomas looks at me.

'They did.'

The men start muttering about how they aren't surprised, that something needs to be done about that Evans boy and his band of thugs.

'Did I hear mention of my son?' Reverend Evans pokes his head around the little crowd.

Some of the men look embarrassed, but one of them, the man called Dai who brought Ronnie's mattress, says, 'Yeah. What've you got to say about him picking on little dwts like Alun's lad?'

The vicar ignores him and goes over to Mr Thomas. 'We only have the boy's word for it, and that doesn't count for much –' his eyes flick towards me – 'given who his older brother is. The more likely explanation is that he's simply been up to mischief.'

Mr Thomas stands and points at Ronnie's arms. 'This is all your boy's doing, Cedwyn.'

'Those bramble scratches?' Reverend Evans almost smiles as he looks at Ronnie's arms, and it's all I can do not to kick him. 'Been picking blackberries, have you, boy?'

'Don't talk to my brother,' I mutter, pulling Ronnie close to me.

He raises his eyebrows. 'I see your manners haven't improved since our last conversation. Yet all's well that ends well. The Good Lord has seen fit to deliver him back to us.'

'Has he now then?' Mr Thomas's voice is hard like steel. 'And who's this *us*? I didn't see *you* out searching for the little lad.'

The vicar has a look on his face that Nan would call 'brazen'. 'I knew he'd be around somewhere – and hasn't he proved me right? Gallivanting all over our mountain while decent people stop their day to search for him. Look at him now, standing there with his hands in his pockets – no respect!'

Ronnie pulls out his hands. I let go of him to shove mine deep into my own.

'Decent people, eh?' Mr Thomas's words come out

with a laugh like a bark. 'That explains why *you* didn't help, then, Evans.'

Florence whistles long and low. The two men stare at each other, real hate in their eyes.

Reverend Evans smiles like a snake that's caught a mouse. 'As I said, the Lord has delivered the lost child safely to you.' He starts to walk away, then turns back and mutters, 'This time.'

This time? What does he mean, *This time*? The men shuffle their feet. Dai says something under his breath that sounds like a word you wouldn't normally say in front of a vicar.

That dark cloud is back, the one that drifted over Mr Thomas the day Florence punched Jack. And now it's got thunder in it. He closes his eyes and takes a really big breath, like he's pushing down the anger, and crouches next to Ronnie again. Then he stands, lifting my brother with him as if he weighs nothing at all. Ronnie clings to his neck, not minding the coal dust, and we walk down to Heol Mabon together.

CHAPTER TWENTY-SEVEN
TRICKS

Ronnie and me walk up from Sunday school with Florence. I didn't listen to a word Miss Williams said, my head's too full of how Reverend Evans and Mr Thomas were with each other. And I can't stop wondering what the reverend meant about Ronnie being safe 'this time'. Or why the men shuffled their feet and looked away. I don't understand this place, these people. Everyone knows everyone else, but there are huge secrets too. Secrets they don't want outsiders like us to know.

We turn the corner on to the Bryn and someone waves at us from across the road. It's Duff. Duff who stood in the Bunker, letting Jack hit my brother with sticks. My fists tighten.

'What does *he* want?' Florence says, screwing up her face and grabbing Ronnie's hand.

I step out ahead of them. 'I don't know but it won't be anything good.'

When I reach the pavement, Duff smiles but it's weak like it's hurting his face to do it. 'All right, Jimmy?'

I say nothing. I want to bring my fist crunching down on his double-crossing face like Florence did to Jack, but a group of women are coming along the pavement. Church people in their Sunday best.

Florence and Ronnie join us. Duff says hello to them and Florence's answer is a rude finger sign. Ronnie goes to copy her but I grab his arm and hold it down at his side. The church ladies gasp and tut and stick their noses in the air.

'Erm,' Duff says, shuffling from foot to foot like he's nervous. 'What Jack did to Ronnie, it was bad. Look at him, he's only a little fella.'

Duff nods towards Ronnie, who stands up straight and tall, puffing out his chest like a sergeant major on parade.

I glare at Duff. 'You were part of it, don't try to make out you weren't.'

'But Jack made me – you don't know what it's like living in that vicarage with him. He bullies me too, you know.'

'You tied up and tortured a six-year-old,' I say, breathing hard. 'Not even living with flaming *Hitler* could make me do that!'

'Yeah,' says Florence, stepping towards him, clearly enjoying the way he flinches.

'I'd hate me too if I was you.' Duff shoves his hands deep into his pockets and looks at the ground. 'I don't want to be in his stupid gang any more. I want us to be mates again … like we used to.'

A little voice in my head starts whispering, even though I don't want it to. *What if he means it? We* did *used to be mates. Best mates. What if he's telling the truth?*

Duff looks right at me. 'I'm sorry, Jimmy.'

And now I know he's lying. Duff never says sorry for anything. Ever. Unless he's trying to pull the wool over someone's eyes.

I feel Florence's and Ronnie's stares, drilling into me, waiting for me to answer. I turn to them. 'You go. Ronnie, tell Mrs Thomas I'll be home for lunch.'

'Dinner,' Ronnie says.

I sigh. 'All right, dinner then.'

'What the heck, Jimmy?' Florence's eyes are bigger and rounder than Ronnie's. 'You don't believe him, do you?'

Duff's looking at the pavement again. I stare at her really hard. 'Trust me,' I mouth.

She frowns, then nods and leads Ronnie away.

'Want to go down to the bottom field?' I ask, watching his face closely. He's trying to look relieved, I know he is, but he just looks smug. This could be a trap, a way to get me on my own and kick my head in. Suddenly I wish I hadn't told Florence to go.

I don't say much. Duff and me sit on the grass and he goes on and on about how horrible Jack is and I pretend to believe him. He starts picking at his nails; I think I'm about to find out what he's up to.

He looks across the field and sighs. 'So what's this about a skull then?'

I knew it.

'What are you talking about? What skull?'

He pulls a bit of nail off his thumb and flicks it into the grass. 'Ronnie said he'd *never tell us about the skull*. Which is funny when you think about it, because that's just what he did, didn't he? Tell us, I mean.'

There's a chance for me to get one over on him here, get one over on them all. If I can only think of a good story. What did Florence say the skull could be? A drunken miner, a Victorian poacher, a German spy … That's it! A German spy.

I try to look like I'm considering telling him. I rub my chin like Dad does when he's thinking hard. I suck the air in through my teeth. I frown a lot.

'I don't know, Duff.' I stare into the distance. I have to make this look like he's dragging it out of me. 'This is big. Top secret, really. *Classified*, you could say.'

He sits bolt upright and nods his head fast. 'Go on – you can trust me.'

I almost laugh but make my face go really serious. I speak quietly and lean nearer to him.

'See, Duff, there was a parachute landing around here over the summer. A German spy acting for Hitler.'

He's bouncing now, all excited.

'Only it didn't go according to plan and he crashed into the side of the mountain. SPLAT!' I clap my hands together and Duff jumps. I'm starting to enjoy this. 'They say his head flew clean off and landed in the stream.'

'*Really*? Is that where it is – in the stream? *Where* in the stream?'

'That's it, isn't it? No one knows, but it'll be just a skull by now with all the weather and animals and things.'

'A real skull? With eyeholes and that creepy bit where the nose used to be and its mouth all …' He clenches his teeth and opens and closes his jaw like a ventriloquist's dummy.

'Err … not really.' I say. 'But … Ronnie was looking for it when you found him.'

'How did he know about it?'

'We overheard some old fellas talking. They stopped when they saw us.'

Duff frowns. 'Hold on, we – I mean Jack – accused Ronnie of being a German spy in the Bunker …'

Oh no, he's going to know I'm making this up. But then he nods slowly and smiles as if he's had a brilliant idea.

'That must've made Ronnie think of the skull. We reminded him of the German parachutist!'

I shrug. 'Must have.'

'What I don't understand, Jimmy,' Duff says, 'is what happened to his body and his parachute.'

Oh heck, what do I say now? I cough, trying to buy some time. *Think, Jimmy, what would Florence say?* Then it comes to me. 'The army sneaked in and cleared up. That's what they do, isn't it? Secret missions.'

Duff puts a hand on my shoulder and pinches it really hard as he pushes himself up off the grass.

'Thanks, Jimmy, you just saved me and the gang a whole lot of bother.' He kicks my shin before he runs away. 'So long, sucker!' he shouts over his shoulder.

I rub my leg but I'm smiling. Takes one to know one.

CHAPTER TWENTY-EIGHT

IT'S GOT TO BE JACK

After feeding our Sunday dinner scraps to the chickens, we knock for Florence and head back up the mountain.

'Do you know what?' she says, jumping down off the gate and marching towards the tree. 'After seeing that diagram, I reckon I could rebuild the bones into a proper skeleton.'

'Don't!' Ronnie squeaks.

She looks back. 'Oh, I won't really do it,' she says, holding out her hand. 'I'm just saying, I think

I'd be a good scientist.'

Ronnie takes her hand and they skip towards the tree.

Under its shade, I pour honey on to the bread that Florence brought and we spread it around with our fingers. No one thought to bring a knife. She passes me a pop bottle filled with water, it's warm but it doesn't matter. Back in London I never would've taken a drink from something she'd touched. I feel my face burn with shame; we used to say there were Campbell Germs on everything. Duff started it one day when Florence had been on a swing in the park. He said anyone who sat on it after her would be infected. Florence waited in the bushes and threw stones at us on our way home. Duff got her into trouble for that.

I can't believe I was ever friends with him.

'So why did you want us to come up here?' Florence asks.

'There's no one nosing around,' I say. 'I'm fed up of half the flaming village thinking I'm a thief. We need to put a stop to it.'

Ronnie licks honey off the back of his hand. 'How?'

'We expose the real culprit—'

Florence opens her mouth but I cut in. 'And yes – before you say it – we all know you'd make a brilliant detective *blah blah blah*, but let me finish ...'

Her mouth snaps shut and she pulls a face.

I ignore her. 'It's got to be Jack. Look at the evidence: he's the one with easy access to the collection money. He hates us. He's sly and spiteful and would love to make evacuees look bad, especially me. I wish we could make people see I'm not the thief as easily as Duff believed there was a parachutist.'

'The trouble is, not everyone around here is as thick as Tommy Duffy,' Florence says.

'There must be a way. Come on, Florence – *you are* good at working things out.'

'Very true.' She gets up and wanders around in front of us, tapping her head and frowning. Oh heck, she's getting silly and dramatic again. She's about three paces away when there's a loud creaking noise from above.

Then a crack.

There's no time to even shout a warning. The branch whacks Florence on top of the head and she hits the ground with a horrible thud.

Ronnie squeals. We leap up and rush to her.

Florence rolls around, holding her ankle. There's blood on her face and a rip in her dress. She's breathing in and out through her teeth but she's not crying. Ronnie is though. On the ground next to her is a really big branch. One end is spiky where it snapped off the tree. How the *heck* did that happen? Ronnie whimpers and drops to his knees, taking her hand. I crouch next to them.

'I'm all right,' she says, waving me away and looking at Ronnie. 'Are you?'

He nods through his tears. 'But you're not, Florence. Your head's bleeding.'

'Oh.' She wipes her fingers over her forehead. 'Where?' She sits up and ducks her head towards me. I scratch around in her hair like the nit nurse and think of all the times it was crawling and jumping. She jerks when I find the cut. It isn't very big but the lump's going to be a whopper.

'You got a hanky?' I ask.

She digs in her pocket and passes it to me. I fold it into a pad.

'Here.' I lay it on top of the cut, take her hand and put her fingers on it. 'Press down.'

'Ow!' She screws up her face. So does Ronnie but at least he's stopped crying.

'Sorry.' I point at the branch. 'Look at the size of that! Florence, you were flipping lucky, then.'

'I don't feel very lucky.' She looks at it, then up at the tree, wincing as she does. There's a sharp, jagged stump poking out of the trunk. 'What happened?'

'I don't know, it just … *broke*.'

'Oh no, no,' she whispers, smoothing out her dress to look at the tear. 'It's ruined.'

'It's not that bad,' I say, getting up. 'It'll patch.'

'I want to go home.'

'She means the shop,' Ronnie says.

'I know,' I say. 'Come on, then.'

'No.' Florence waves an arm at the bottle and bread bag. 'Pick up our rubbish first.'

Crikey, even when she's bleeding, she's bossy.

Ronnie grabs them as Florence tries to stand, but she only just gets off the ground. Her knees buckle and she's back down again. I hold out my hand. She takes it and I help her up.

'You're going to have to lean on me,' I say. 'Put your arm round my shoulders.'

Florence looks more horrified than when she first held the skull. I try to give her a hard stare, like she does to me, but it just makes her laugh. I let go and she wobbles on one leg.

'Look,' I say, getting fed up now. 'Either put your arm round my shoulders or hop down this flaming mountain on your own.'

CHAPTER TWENTY-NINE

A PROPER EGG

It takes us ages to reach Florence's street. We pass Jack's mother and Miss Goodhew; they're on the other side of the Bryn and don't cross it to help. Instead they watch us with suspicion.

'Is there a lump yet?' I ask. 'Let's have a look.'

Florence stops and lifts the hanky. It sticks a bit with the drying blood. 'Ooow.'

'Blimey, it's a proper egg!'

She puts the hanky back over the wound and I think about how fast that branch fell. There was no warning, just a bit of a creak, and BAM! It hit her.

Florence frowns and ferrets about in her hair.

'What's the matter?' I say.

'M-m-my ribbon!' She splutters like an old engine. 'My ribbon's gone!'

'Is that all? I thought your head was splitting open or something.'

'I have to find it.' She turns quickly and wobbles again. Good job I've got her.

'What are you doing? It's only a ribbon.'

Her face crumples. 'I've never had a ribbon before.'

'But you live in a shop, there must be miles of ribbon in there! I bet Phyllis will let you have a new one.'

'You don't understand – I want *my* ribbon.'

'All right, if you two can get to the shop from here *I'll* go back,' I say. 'Blimey, Florence, sometimes you can be such a *girl*.'

Florence's ribbon is where she fell, next to the branch and the blood. I slip it into my pocket and head back.

I haven't got far when I spot three boys further down the mountain, wading through the stream. A smaller, skinnier boy stands on the bank, waving his arms about and looking fed up.

Jack and his gang.

I duck behind a clump of bushes. It's obvious Jack's giving orders. Gareth and Aled are bending over, sweeping their arms around in the water as if they've lost their soap in the bath. Duff's shuffling around near the bank, staring hard into the stream.

Suddenly there's a shout and a huge splash as Gareth disappears, resurfacing a second later, drenched and shaking his head like a dog.

I try not to laugh too loud.

'I can't see! I can't see!' Gareth wails. 'The German must have put poison in the water!'

'You've lost your glasses, you idiot!' Jack shouts.

'Aww, Gar,' Aled yells, 'Mam's gunna kill you!'

I leave Jack and his gang arguing over whether it's more important to find the skull of a German parachutist or Gareth's specs.

*

I run along the street and into the shop. Ieuan's behind the counter.

'Mam's got Dr Jenkins here,' he says, waving me through. 'They're in the kitchen.'

Florence sits on a chair with her leg up on a pouffe, sipping from a steaming mug. Ronnie's on the rug in front of the range with Noble.

'Look, Jimmy!' He beams, holding up his own mug. 'Fancy having Horlicks in the daytime!'

The doctor shines a little torch into Florence's eyes. 'A branch fell on you, you say?'

She nods, then winces.

Phyllis comes in with some cushions and puts them behind Florence's back. She smiles at me. 'I'll do you a Horlicks now in a minute. Just getting my girl comfy first.'

'Her pupils are fine, Phyllis,' Dr Jenkins says, 'but you'll have to watch out for concussion. Don't let her drop off for the next few hours and if she gets really sleepy, feels sick or has a bad headache then call me.'

'Thank you, Doctor. It's so good of you to come out on a Sunday.'

'Not at all.' He smiles at Florence, then glances at the ribbon in my hand. 'That'll need a boil wash before it goes near that wound. Germs, see.'

'Jimmy, you found it!' Florence looks like I brought her a diamond, not a dirty, bloody ribbon.

Phyllis spoons powder into a mug. 'You're a good boy, Jimmy.'

Florence takes the ribbon and grins at me. 'He's not bad.'

'Wych elms do that, you know.' Ieuan's leaning against the door frame. 'Drop their branches without warning.'

'There's a witch?' Ronnie squeaks.

'Not witch like a spooky witch.' Ieuan laughs and waggles his fingers. 'W-Y-C-H. Was it a wych elm?'

I shrug.

'Did the leaves have jagged edges?'

Phyllis hands me my Horlicks. 'Honestly, Ieuan, how are they supposed to know? The girl's lucky she doesn't have a big dent in her skull and you're on about leaves!'

Florence looks at me and I know what she's thinking. This might be a very big clue.

CHAPTER THIRTY

NYE

Mrs Thomas stirs sugar into a big mug of tea. She wipes her forehead with the back of her hand and sighs. I think she's still upset about Ronnie going missing. Since we rescued him, Mr Thomas has been spending even more time in the garden and not saying much. Maybe it's too much trouble to have us here after all.

'Is that for Mr Thomas?' I ask, putting down the letter I'm writing to Dad and Nan. 'I'll take it out to him.'

I have to do this for my little brother's sake. I have

to know what Reverend Evans meant about Ronnie being safe 'this time'. Even though there's no way Jack will get him again. Not with Florence and me to watch out for him.

Mrs Thomas hands the mug to me. She looks tired. 'That's very kind. Thank you, Jimmy. Then I can get on with the cleaning.'

'Ronnie'll help,' I say. He looks up from the floor, where he's driving his Dinky van in and out of the chair legs.

'But I'm making a racetrack,' he says.

'That can wait. Earn your keep.'

She smiles at me and mouths, 'Thank you.' I smile back.

Mr Thomas said he was going out to earth up the leeks but he's sitting on the bench now, his hands black from the soil. Mrs Thomas never gets at him for his dirty nails like Mum used to get at Dad. He's looking up at the mountain.

'I brought you a cuppa.' I'm glad of something to say, something to cut through the odd feeling hanging in the air.

'Good lad.'

Mr Thomas takes the mug. I don't move.

'Want something, boy?' he says.

Say it, Jimmy. Just ask him. 'What are they?' I point at the dark green leaves of the potato plants. *Stupid.*

Mr Thomas frowns and half smiles. 'Potatoes. Same as they were when you dug some up for your tea last night.'

I grind my shoe into the path.

'What do you really want?' he asks, tapping the bench next to him. I sit. He drinks and waits.

I stare straight ahead as if vegetables are the most fascinating things in the world. 'What did Reverend Evans mean when he said "this time"? He said Ronnie was safe *this time*.'

Mr Thomas runs a finger around the rim of his mug. 'He said that, did he?'

'Yes.' I stop myself from saying *You know he did*. 'Was it a threat?'

He looks shocked. 'Pardon?'

'He said "this time" like there'd be a next time, that

Ronnie might not come back *next time*. Like Jack will kidnap him again and we won't get him back!'

'No, no, it's nothing like that. Cedwyn Evans isn't a good man. But even he wouldn't allow …' Mr Thomas draws in a big breath and holds it for a long time. 'It was a dig at me. You see, I had a little brother.'

I sit up and stare right at him.

'Nye, his name was. Short for Aneurin, you know.'

I don't.

'But it was a bit of a mouthful so we called him Nye.'

'I didn't know you had a brother.'

'He went missing when we were boys.'

Suddenly, horribly, I understand what Reverend Evans meant. 'Did he come home?'

Mr Thomas's words are like a sigh. 'No, Jimmy, he didn't come home.'

'Not ever?'

'Not ever.'

A beetle crawls along the arm of the bench. I watch it and wait for Mr Thomas to tell me what happened.

'We were typical brothers,' Mr Thomas says. 'Closer

in age than you and Ronnie though. I was three when Nye was born. He was really funny – always made me laugh, he did, even if I was in a bad mood. He was a happy little thing.'

'Like Ronnie,' I say.

He nods. 'We didn't have much money, like most people round here, so big presents had to be shared. One Christmas, I think I must have been about seven or eight, we got a tin soldier set.' Mr Thomas twists his wedding ring on his finger. 'I looked after the set really well and made sure all the figures were back in their box every night. I understood how many extra shifts our dad had worked to pay for it, see. Nye, well, he wasn't so careful.'

'Did he break it?'

'No, but he took a shine to the drummer and used to play with it on its own. Sometimes he couldn't remember where he'd left it, and there'd be a big hoo-ha in our house while everyone hunted for it, but we managed to keep the set nice for years.'

'Ronnie lost his Dinky van on holiday once – that's why he isn't allowed to take it outside.'

'A sensible rule.' Mr Thomas takes one last big swig of tea and puts his mug on the bench. 'Then, one afternoon after rugby training, I heard noises coming from the coal bunker. I wasn't surprised to find Nye in there – he had a habit of curling up in small spaces when he was tired or upset. Our mam would often find him asleep in the ottoman, or under a chair, wrapped up in that candlewick bedspread from your room.'

He shakes his head and smiles in a sad way.

'Black as the night he was. I can still see the streaks down his face where his crying had washed off the coal dust. He'd taken the little toy drummer up the mountain and on the way home it'd poured with rain so he ran. When he got home it wasn't in his pocket.'

'Were you cross?' I ask.

Mr Thomas rubs his eyes. 'I dragged him out, coal dust and all, and made him retrace his steps. Up and down we went, till he'd cried off most of the dust and my temper was higher than the top of the mountain. By now it was past teatime but I told him to keep looking while I went home. Sausage and mash, it was …'

He blinks.

'I never saw him again. Weeks later, when the police had almost given up searching and my mam's heart was broken beyond fixing, a really young constable knocked our door. I watched from the stairs. He didn't say anything, just handed Nye's cap to my father. My mam's legs gave way and my father caught her as she fell into a dead faint. That was the end of it. No more searching. The police said he must have run away, that they'd have found a body by now. That finished my mam, that did, the word "body".'

I don't know what to say so I just stare at the vegetables again.

'But he wouldn't have run away, I know that much. Yeah, we argued that day, but it wasn't *unusual*. Like I said, typical brothers. It wasn't enough to make him leave. The police got that wrong.'

Now things make sense; the way Mr Thomas ran out all dirty and scared when Ronnie was missing. What Reverend Evans said.

'Do you think Nye's still alive?' I ask, hoping like mad, wishing so hard for it to be true.

He hangs his head, his voice a low mumble. 'Can't see how he can be, not after all this time.'

I feel like I want to reach out, pat his arm or something. But I don't.

He turns to face me, his eyes watery. Black coals in little pools. 'It's the not knowing that gets you, Jimmy. I just want to know he's at peace.' He sees my confused look. 'Oh, not in heaven or that sort of thing. Just that his … his *remains* … aren't in a ditch somewhere. I can't stand the thought of him all alone in the place where he died.'

I take a big breath. 'So when Reverend Evans said that about Ronnie, he was talking about Nye?'

I can't believe anyone could be so cruel.

'He was. Cedwyn Evans doesn't like people who don't think the way he does. And you already know I'm not the God-fearing type. My mam was though. She'd always gone to St Michael's, always said her prayers.'

'St Michael's? I thought your family would be chapel, like Mrs Thomas.'

He smiles but it looks tight and makes his lips thin. 'Church, chapel … Didn't make a difference though, did it? It didn't bring my brother home. That's when Mam stopped going, lost her faith completely. The vicar at the time respected that, left us alone with our grief, but when Cedwyn arrived it was a different story. He took against us straight away because Mam left the church, said we were sinners. So when he heard about Nye he saw that as his opportunity to have a go.'

Anger at Reverend Evans bubbles inside me but I say nothing.

'It isn't difficult in a place like this to start up rumours. Especially when the rumours are about the Thomases.' He must see the look on my face because he almost laughs. 'You must have heard them talking, Jimmy. Seen the looks they give us. In this valley, being a Thomas is a bad thing to some people. Do you remember what I said about black sheep and Florence's family?'

I nod, feeling my cheeks burn.

'Well, we aren't so different, me and Flossie. It's hard though, to shake off a tag like that. Especially round here when a preacher's the one making sure it keeps going.'

I think about what the women said at the welcome party – *If the reverend says so, it must be true*.

'Cedwyn has always made out that I had something to do with my brother going missing.'

'That's terrible!'

'It is. But it doesn't matter what anyone else says, really. They can't punish me more than I punish myself. I made Nye stay up there.'

'Mr Thomas, it's not your fault!'

He shakes his head and I want to put my arms around him like I did with Dad after Mum left.

Now all the other things start to fit together – how some people frowned when Mrs Thomas chose us, the two old fellas arguing in Welsh, the way Mrs Ringrose is to Mrs Thomas, Mr Thomas not going to John Ringrose's funeral. It all makes horrible sense.

He picks up his mug and stands. 'Well, I'd better get off to work. No rest for the wicked, eh?'

He stops and looks back at me. 'Thanks, Jimmy.'

'Mrs Thomas made your tea,' I say.

'I didn't mean the tea.'

CHAPTER THIRTY-ONE

SMALL SPACES

The thought buzzes in my mind like a trapped bee. I rush through the kitchen and living room, down the passage and out on to the pavement. Because there's only one way to be sure.

I run, not knowing if my feet or my heart pounds hardest and loudest.

I need to know.

I need to know.

Mr Thomas needs to know.

Down Heol Mabon, across the Bryn, along the

next street and over the fence.

Then up the mountain to the tree. If there's an answer, that's where it'll be.

But at the gate I stop, suddenly afraid to be right. I think of Mr Thomas again and force myself on.

Kneeling at the hollow, my skin prickles hot and cold. There's the skull, where I left it. I move it to one side and crawl forward. No waiting. No messing about or I won't do it.

I stick my head right in. Darkness. A small space. *Breathe, Jimmy.* Coolness. Moss smells and earth smells and nutty wood smells. My eyes get used to the dark.

I blink a few times.

Shapes appear. Whiteness at the back of the hollow. And then I see.

Bones. Not like in the diagram, all neat and ordered. Instead, like sticks in an odd-shaped pile. If I think too hard about who it might be I want to cry, because I don't know if I even want this to be true. I pat my hand around but there's nothing that feels like …

Something scratches against my palm. My fingers close around a tiny, hard object.

Out in the light again, I sit back and open my hand.

It's made of metal and caked in dried mud. I rub and pick at it. I smooth off the dirt until colours show through. Red. Black.

I run down to the stream and hold it in the water and rub it again. A red uniform. A tall black hat. A tin soldier playing a drum.

I turn the little figure over and over in my hand. It's like I'm falling head first into a deep, dark hole, my mind spinning. Nye liked small spaces; he could have crawled inside the hollow. The bones are him. They have to be.

'We knew you'd be here.'

I jump and look up to see Florence and Ronnie walking towards me. She's hobbling a bit.

My fingers close around the little tin drummer. 'How did you get up here on that ankle?'

'It wasn't even a sprain. Phyllis bandaged it anyway and – What are you holding?'

I open my hand to show the toy soldier lying on my

palm. 'I think I know who it is.' My voice is loud but wobbly. 'In the tree.'

Florence stares at the drummer, her voice wobbly too. 'It's not a *child* in there, is it?'

I tap the grass next to me, like Mr Thomas did with the bench. We sit close together on the bank and I tell them everything he told me. When I get to the part about Nye in the coal bunker, Florence starts to cry. Ronnie looks confused but holds her hand anyway and neither of them says a word. Nothing. Which makes it even harder somehow.

When I've finished, Florence wipes her face with the back of her hand. 'You have to tell Alun,' she says.

'I know.' I feel sick at the thought. 'I'll tell him tonight when he gets in from work.'

We get up and I put the drummer in my pocket.

'Sausage and mash,' she whispers.

'Pardon?'

Florence's eyes fill up again. She blinks and a big tear drops on to her cheek. 'Imagine having a day in your life so bad you remember exactly what you had for tea.'

CHAPTER THIRTY-TWO

PULLING TOGETHER

I keep my hand pressed tight to my pocket as we set off down the mountain, keeping the toy soldier safe. Suddenly a sound like dogs being tortured wails through the valley.

'Is it an air raid?' Ronnie asks, his eyes wide and terrified.

'It can't be,' I say, but my heart is thumping fast. 'They sent us here to be safe.' I look up but all I can see are clouds. Perhaps the bombers are flying above them?

'Jimmy,' Florence says, her face white as a sheet.

'I know!' I shout over the siren. 'We need to get to a shelter.'

'No.' She's shaking her head really fast, staring over the valley.

'It's not an air raid. It's the pit siren.'

The pit.

All those men down there.

Mr Thomas down there.

We run like the devil himself is after us, down past the graveyard, along the footpath and out on to the streets.

More than once, Florence stumbles and almost goes over on her ankle but just waves an arm and shouts back at us, 'I'm fine!'

We reach the top of the Bryn and stop. I've never seen so many people out at once here. For a second it's like being back in London. Small groups of men hurry upwards, larger groups of women stand around in headscarves, patting each other on the arm or offering to put the kettle on. Others move downwards. We join them but it's like we're invisible. Three evacuated ghosts walking slowly through the Llanbryn people.

Another wail. A long, low tone but different to the pit siren. An ambulance speeds past us, up the hill.

Florence and me share a panicked look over the top of Ronnie's head.

Then a bell clangs through the din. 'It's a fire engine, Jimmy,' Ronnie whispers. He wriggles his fingers into my hand, looking scared, not excited like he usually would.

Someone bumps into me as they rush past. It's Ieuan. I reach and grab his sleeve.

'What's happening?' I ask.

'Cave-in.'

My whole body tingles and my head whooshes like it's underwater. Mr Thomas could be hurt or … I push the thought out of my head. 'What can we do?'

'Nothing,' he says, walking away backwards. 'Just … keep out of the way.'

'Ieuan, we can't do nothing!' Florence says, her voice choked.

He ruffles her hair, like people do to Ronnie. 'Then go to the institute and find Mam. People are rallying there.' He sets off again, lost in the crowd.

We run. Down and down and down to the Miners Institute. No one sees us. The siren howls and moans.

It's like the operations room of a war film. With Mr Bevan as the general. He stands in the middle of the hall telling people where to put tables and what to put on them. Nearest the door are some older men, including Dai, crowded together holding bits of paper. Women carry tray after tray of cups and saucers and plates and put them near the stage. Phyllis and Mrs Jenkins lift a big urn on to a table. Florence goes to them. The two old fellas I met when I was looking for the shop are talking to some policemen.

Even Mrs Ringrose and Mrs Evans are moving chairs.

I don't see Mrs Thomas until Ronnie gasps and runs across the hall. He tries to wrap his arms around her, but it's like she doesn't know he's there. She tucks a bit of hair into her headscarf and rushes off. I go to him.

'She didn't want a cuddle,' he says quietly.

I take his hand and lead him over to Florence and Phyllis.

'Where's Mr Thomas?' I ask.

'Oh my poor little dabs.' Phyllis takes our hands. 'He's at the colliery.'

'But he's all right?' I say. 'He's out?'

She glances towards the door. 'We're waiting for news. Dai's organising runners to keep us updated.'

'But he'll be all right, won't he? They all will.'

'No one's above ground yet but … look … I need you to go back to the shop.'

'We're not leaving you,' Florence says, taking her hand. 'We want to help.'

'We could do with some washer-uppers once these cups and plates get dirty,' Mrs Jenkins says, trying to smile. 'The children can sit on the stage out of the way till then. Can't they?'

Phyllis rubs her forehead. 'Oh, I suppose so.'

Florence and Ronnie sit down but I can't keep still. I pace back and forth in front of them.

'They'll get them all out,' I say. 'This probably happens all the time.'

'It doesn't, Jimmy.' Florence's voice is a croaky sort of whisper. 'Phyllis said they only sound the siren if it's really bad. Smaller rockfalls are a part of mining, they're used to them. This is … really bad.'

My stomach knots up. 'He's going to be all right.'

'Of course he is.' Florence puts her hand on my sleeve. I jerk it away, wrap my arms around myself and keep pacing.

CHAPTER THIRTY-THREE

RAT CATCHING

There's a big commotion in the middle of the hall. Mr Bevan is trying to calm Jack's mother and Mrs Ringrose, who are waving their arms around and throwing nasty looks our way. I catch some of their words. *Cash box. Money. Thieves*.

Mr Bevan clears his throat. 'Good people of Llanbryn, if I may have your attention for just a moment …' He's so loud, everyone stops at once. 'We seem to have had a bit of a … erm … *mishap* regarding the miners' benevolent fund cash box. If we

N

can all search our areas, Mrs Evans and I will have another look through the drawers.'

'I've told you, Ceri. I had it locked in that drawer in the downstairs office and the key's missing too!' Mrs Evans argues. 'And I think we all know who's to blame, don't we? It's been the same ever since those children came from London.'

Phyllis and Mrs Jenkins look like they're about to explode. Then Mrs Thomas comes from nowhere and marches into the middle of the hall. 'Got any proof, Ruth?'

Mr Bevan holds up his hands. 'Now now, ladies. Let's all calm down. I'm sure there's a rational explanation that *doesn't* involve casting blame.'

A dark muttering goes around the hall, full of words like *evacuees*, *Thomas family* and *bad eggs*. All eyes are on us now. Florence stands, puts her hands on her hips and gives them all a very bad stare. I know it isn't helping but I'm still pleased she's doing it.

I feel a tug on my sleeve. 'What's a cash box?' Ronnie whispers.

'A box to keep money in,' I say. 'A tin one with a lock.'

Ronnie frowns. 'Can it fit in a gas mask box?'

'Depends. Why?'

Ronnie points at a slightly open door at the back of the hall, just behind the stage. Standing there is Jack Evans.

Looking shifty.

His head flicks from side to side and he's holding his gas mask box tight to his body.

I glance around; all the grown-ups are fussing and flapping and searching for the missing cash box. No one's noticed Jack edging towards the main doors of the hall.

'Come on,' I whisper to Florence and Ronnie. 'Let's see what he's up to.'

I step in front of Jack, knowing they're right behind me. 'What's in there, Evans?' I say, poking the gas mask box. It makes an odd jingling sound.

'Nothing.' Jack holds it closer.

'It's the cash box, isn't it?' Florence says.

'What's it to you, shunk? My mother asked me

to fetch it. She knows it isn't safe with *vaccies* around.'

'Liar.'

He must know he's been rumbled because he says, 'Let me go or I'll tell everyone you stole it and I was trying to stop you.'

'Get stuffed,' I say.

'Yeah, get stuffed,' repeats Ronnie.

Jack laughs. 'And who do you think everyone will believe? You three vaccies – or the vicar's son?'

'Shut your mouth, Jack Evans!' Ronnie almost shouts.

'Or what? You'll run to Alun Thomas and *tell on me*? Be a bit difficult if he's *dead*.'

It's like a twig snapping in my head and I launch a swing at him but he's ready. He dodges and makes for the door. But before he gets past Phyllis's table, Ronnie pushes him hard from behind.

Jack flies into the middle of the hall, putting out his hands to save himself. The string snaps and his gas mask box lands on the floor with a thud and a jangle of metal. It opens, and a black-and-gold tin box tumbles out. Jack scrabbles to pick it up but it's too late.

The fussing and flapping and searching stops. All is quiet. Everyone's eyes are on him.

'No! Wait! It was *them*!' He points at Florence, Ronnie and me. 'They're the thieves. I was stopping them.'

'Nonsense!' Mr Bevan shouts, and it's a very different sound to his happy boom. 'These children have been in the hall the entire time.'

People in the crowd mutter and nod.

'But you have to believe me.' Jack looks around as if he doesn't understand. 'They're filthy vaccies!'

Even Mrs Ringrose gasps.

The crowd splits and Reverend Evans sweeps through. His eyes are tiny slits; his voice is a terrifying roar. 'Jack Tudor Evans! HOME! NOW!'

CHAPTER THIRTY-FOUR

ALUN THOMAS'S BOY

I had to get out of there. Any other time I would have loved to listen to everyone saying what a rotten egg Jack Evans is, to see the shame on the faces of those who thought it was me. But not today. Not with the cave-in and the fear and the panic that I won't ever get to tell Mr Thomas where his brother is.

I lean on the fence at the end of the street, staring at the fields that lead to the tree. It was here Florence first told me she was Ieuan's sister and I thought she was mad. And I thought he was mad for letting her. Now she's my best friend, so I suppose that makes me mad too. But I wouldn't swap her for a thousand Duffs.

I take the tin soldier out of my pocket and march it along the top of the fence, just like Ronnie might. My little brother never had a problem fitting in. I used to think it was because he's cute, but the truth is, people like the Thomases and Phyllis and Ieuan make it easy. If you let them.

It's so much better here than I ever thought it could be. But what if it all changes? What if …

I grip the drummer so hard it digs into my hand.

There's a noise in the street and I turn to see a man putting a key into his front door. He stops, looks up, then jogs over. It's Dai.

'You all right there?' he calls. 'Oh, you're Alun Thomas's boy, aren't you?'

I nod.

'Then I've got some news,' he pants. 'Coming from the institute I am now …'

Please God, let him be alive.

'... Alun's all right. Bit bashed up like, but he'll mend.'

My whole body goes soft. I grip the fence to stop me falling.

'If you go now, you might catch Gwen before she leaves for the—'

But I'm already running.

When I get to the institute, a man's helping Mrs Thomas into a car, then he walks around and gets in the driver's seat. He starts the engine and pulls away. I stop on the pavement, panting and holding my side.

Phyllis, Florence and Ronnie are in the arched doorway, waving her off.

'Jimmy!' Ronnie shouts. 'Where were you? He's safe! Uncle Alun's safe!'

'I know, Dai told me.' I walk over and put my arms around him.

'Your Aunty Gwen has gone to the hospital,' Phyllis says. 'They've taken Alun to be checked over so she's gone to be with him.'

'Will they come home tonight?' Ronnie asks.

'No, bach. You're staying with us. Take pillows and blankets into the living room and all be together. That's important at a time like this.' Phyllis takes Ronnie's face in her hands and squeezes his cheeks. 'I'll come up as soon as I can. Off you go now, there's still men unaccounted for.' She must see the confused looks on our faces. 'Missing.'

We say goodbye and walk back up the hill.

In Phyllis's living room, we snuggle under our blankets. Ronnie's asleep straight away. He doesn't even ask for his Dinky van. There's a scuffling sound at the door and Noble noses his way in. He flops on top of Florence with a happy grunt.

'Hello, boy,' she whispers.

'Aren't you squashed?' I ask.

'A bit. But it's nice, like an extra blanket.'

'Bit smelly though.'

'No smellier than you.' She giggles. 'Turn the lamp off, Travers. There's a war on, you know.'

CHAPTER THIRTY-FIVE

A THOUGHT

Mr and Mrs Thomas are in the parlour. The feeling that I need to talk to him swells inside me like a balloon. I have to tell him about the bones before it bursts, but I can't.

She won't let us see him yet. She said he needs to recuperate in peace and, anyway, he's sad because two of his workmates died and four more are still in hospital. Mr Thomas was in for three days with cracked ribs and cuts and bruises but wouldn't stay any longer. He said he needed home, not hospital.

Ronnie offered to tell him jokes to cheer him up but Mrs Thomas said it wasn't a good idea. Probably best; he only knows daft ones that no one else laughs at.

Now we're washing up after tea. We had corned beef cawl because there wasn't any lamb, but Mrs Thomas said it still had a lot of goodness in for a recovering patient and two growing boys. I thought it was really nice; the way the corned beef mixed through the stew, going all squishy and soaking up the juices. I might even like it better than real cawl.

Ronnie puts the last spoon on the draining board and gets down off his step.

'Want to play snakes and ladders?' he asks. I nod.

We're just at the end of the third game – the decider – when Mrs Thomas comes through to the living room. She looks tired but she's smiling.

'Can we see Uncle Alun now?' Ronnie asks.

She kneels between us on the rug. 'Good boys, you are.' She puts her arms around both of us and it feels right to lean into her like Ronnie does. 'He's asleep. If he has a good night, you can go in in the morning.'

She sits up straight. 'Now, who's winning?'

'Me,' Ronnie says.

'I'll make us all some Horlicks,' Mrs Thomas says. 'Then a story, then bed. It's been a long few days.'

She reads us *Winnie-the-Pooh*. After a few pages, Christopher Robin comes out from behind a green door in a tree.

'Does he live in there?' Ronnie asks, pointing to the picture.

'I suppose he must,' Mrs Thomas says. 'Imagine that.'

'What does he do in there?'

'The same as we do in a house, I suppose … Now where was I?'

'Does he have tea and listen to the wireless?'

'I expect so,' she says.

'And play snakes and ladders?'

'Perhaps.' She lifts the book a bit higher. 'If you let me carry on we'll find out.'

'What would happen if he died in there? Would anyone find him?'

'Ronnie!' I say. It comes out really sharp, and

Mrs Thomas looks at me. I take a breath. 'Don't talk about death like that.'

Ronnie's eyes fill with tears. 'Sorry, Aunty Gwen,' he whispers.

'It's all right,' she says, running her hand over his cowlick. 'It's bound to be on your mind. These are terrible times, with the cave-in and the war.'

Ronnie has that look on his face, the one that says he's fighting the urge to tell. I can't let him. Mr Thomas needs to know first, and he needs to hear it from me.

'I know what will take his mind off it,' I say, desperate to change the subject. 'Ronnie can recite his favourite poem. It's by the same writer.'

Ronnie frowns. 'Is it?'

'Don't you recognise the pictures? They look the same.'

'Oh yes. All right then.' Ronnie stands and smooths down his shirt.

I turn to Mrs Thomas. 'He knows it off by heart.'

He looks right at us and clears his throat, reminding me of Mr Bevan standing in the Miners Institute on our first day here.

'"A Thought", by A.A. Milne,' he says.

The poem is quite silly – which is why he loves it. All about how he'd be six if he was his brother, and not having his own trousers on. He remembers it all.

When he's finished, Mrs Thomas and me clap quietly so we don't wake Mr Thomas. Ronnie takes a deep bow, still chuckling. Then she laughs and it starts me off. Ronnie recites the poem again, this time really showing off and putting in actions till we're all wiping tears of laughter from our faces.

Mrs Thomas tells him to stop when he tries to take his trousers off.

'Oh, Ronnie Travers, you are a tonic,' she says.

I take the mugs into the kitchen and turn on the tap. Mrs Thomas appears in the doorway. 'Leave them to me, bach. You get up that wooden hill after your brother.'

'My nan says that,' I say.

She smiles.

We hear soft, slow thuds from the staircase above us. Ronnie's trying to move quietly. I pull a face. 'He's like a baby elephant.'

'Don't worry, I expect Alun's outers by now.' She slips past me and turns off the tap. 'Night, Jimmy,' she says.

I get as far as the living room, stop and look back at her. I go to say it but the words won't come out.

'Everything all right, bach?' she says.

I nod. *Just say it, Jimmy, it's only words*. I take a deep breath. 'Night, Aunty Gwen.'

She gives a little gasp and blinks. Her face scrunches up a bit. She turns away and waves me off with her dishcloth.

CHAPTER THIRTY-SIX

THERE WERE BONES

Uncle Alun's in the garden and Aunty Gwen's taken Ronnie for an after-breakfast push on the swings. It has to be now. When I go out he looks up from the bench; his eyes are dull, like dusty coal, but he smiles.

For a second I think I can't do it but my feet lead me to the bench. I sit.

'All right, boy?' He coughs. It must hurt because he holds his ribs. 'I'm hoping a bit of fresh air will help clear my lungs.'

'Does it hurt?'

'I'll mend. I'm luckier than some.' He frowns down at the ground. 'I know why you're here.'

It feels like there's no breath in me to speak. Who saw us?

'You want to know about the cave-in, don't you?'

I nod, even though it's not why I'm here.

Uncle Alun carries on. 'I heard about you all wandering the streets and refusing to go to the shop like you were told.'

'I wanted to help but no one would let me.'

'You're a good lad,' he says.

'What *was* it like … down there?'

'If I believed in hell I'd say that was it.' He leans back and closes his eyes. 'I always knew coal mining was a harsh, dangerous job but I never *really* felt it. I'd heard men talk but you just can't imagine it till you're there, that deep under the ground with no way out.'

'I don't like small spaces,' I admit. 'They make me feel dizzy.'

'Don't be a collier then, boy. Don't be a collier.'

Uncle Alun opens his eyes, looks down and twists his wedding ring on his finger. 'I was working a seam – that's where we dig out the coal – when there was an almighty crash and lots of shouting. The ground above us just gave way, the props didn't support it and the ceiling was a big pile of rocks at my feet. It was hard to breathe at first due to all the dust and dirt in the air. Then the lamp on my helmet went out. Pitch dark it was. I was scared. And I'm not ashamed to admit it, either. Scared witless.'

'I was scared when we had to come here,' I say.

'And rightly so. Big thing, evacuation is, all the not knowing, everything so new. Can make a boy angry too, especially if his little brother settles really quick.'

My cheeks burn hot. 'I don't feel like that any more.'

'I know. Your Aunty Gwen said you would come around, said all you needed was kindness and patience.'

She has been kind. And patient. I feel a bit rotten.

I pull at a loose thread on my trousers, wrapping it

round and round till the end of my finger is dark pink. *Do it, Jimmy. Say it.* 'I know where he is.'

'Where who is?' Uncle Alun frowns.

I want to say 'Nye' but it won't come.

I reach inside my pocket. I don't know how I do it but I look him right in the eye and hold out my hand. The tin soldier sits in my palm, shaking as I shake. Uncle Alun looks like I just hit him in the stomach.

He says nothing, just stares and stares. Every second that crawls past feels like forever. He takes a big breath as if he's going to say something, but it makes him hold his ribs and cough.

When he does speak, his voice is a whisper. 'Go on then.'

That's all he says.

'There were bones …'

He blinks. I carry on.

'… hidden inside a hollow tree. At first I didn't know whose they were. I was scared and I ran away, but afterwards I kept going back. Ronnie found out, and then I told Florence.'

He nods, his eyes scrunched up small and tight. I take it as a sign to go on.

'We've been trying to work it all out … what happened … who it is.' My mouth is so dry. I want to swallow but there's nothing there. 'I think … I think … a branch might have hit Nye. It happened to Florence too, at the same tree, only Nye's branch must have been heavier. I think he must have gone in the tree afterwards – you said he liked small spaces. Dr Jenkins told Florence not to go to sleep in case she had concussion. Maybe Nye just went to sleep.'

'A branch,' he whispers.

I twist the loose thread till it snaps off my trousers.

'Then … then … you told me about Nye and it all made sense. But I had to check, so I went in the hollow and I looked and … I found this.' I hold up the drummer.

Silence. I don't know what it means.

'I knew I had to tell you and I was going to, honest, but then the cave-in happened.'

'Where's the tree?' he asks quietly.

I describe the way to the wych elm and how it sits on its own in a field near the stream.

He nods slowly. 'I know it.'

Uncle Alun doesn't take his eyes off the mountain. 'I should have looked harder. I went home for tea, Jimmy. I went home for sausage and flaming mash.'

I offer him the tin soldier. 'It's not your fault.'

He stares at me, tears making his coal-black eyes shinier than ever. Then he looks down at the soldier and takes it, closing his fingers around it. I put my hand on Uncle Alun's arm and he puts his over the top, the soldier pressed between us. His hand is so big that mine completely disappears.

I blink back tears. 'If I lost Ronnie, I don't know what I'd do.'

'Then make the most of him now.'

We sit for a while, not saying anything more. Thinking of our little brothers.

CHAPTER THIRTY-SEVEN

YELLOW FLOWERS

Ronnie, Florence and me sit on the gate and look out over the valley. We had no choice but to come out; Uncle Alun told me to take Ronnie and call for Florence so he could talk to Aunty Gwen.

So we've come to the tree.

I point at the hedgerow further down the field. 'Ronnie, why don't you go and see what flowers are down there? There's a big patch of yellow – Aunty Gwen might like sunny ones.'

'You calling her Gwen now?' Florence says, her

mouth twitching into a smile. I shrug. She grins, and turns to Ronnie. 'I'll help you pick them.'

I kick her and she gives me a look filled with thunder. Ronnie jumps down and runs off.

'What was *that* for?' she says, rubbing her leg like it wasn't just a tap.

'I didn't want to say in front of him.' I point at Ronnie, who's running downhill so fast I think only the hedge will stop him. 'We might not be here much longer.'

'Why? Where are you going?'

'Home. London, I mean. Maybe.'

'For a visit?'

I shake my head. 'For good. Or until we're sent somewhere else.'

'What? Why?'

'Uncle Alun is telling Aunty Gwen about Nye right now. What if we did the wrong thing? What if they don't want us any more?'

I tell her about giving Nye's soldier to Uncle Alun.

'They won't send you away, Jimmy. You *helped* them. You found Nye.'

I feel sick. What if they do send us away? I didn't want to come here but I can't stand the thought of starting all over again with different people, perhaps without mountains and definitely without Florence.

She scrapes the heels of her shoes against the gate. 'Well, he wasn't cross, was he? Just sad. They won't send you back, I'm sure they won't.' She nudges my arm. 'Keep calm and carry on, Private Travers.'

Two people are coming towards us. It's Uncle Alun and Aunty Gwen, their arms around each other's waists. He's carrying a sack and they're looking right at me.

My heart thumps so hard it might burst out of my chest.

This is it.

We're getting sent away again.

'Where's your brother?' Aunty Gwen asks. She doesn't sound angry.

'Down there.' I point, but Ronnie's spotted them and is running back up.

I catch Uncle Alun's eye. He gives a little nod. 'All right, boy?' he says, and I know we're staying.

Relief floods through my body like a warm wave.

Ronnie reaches us, a bunch of yellow flowers in his hand. He gives them to Aunty Gwen. She takes them and kisses the top of his head.

'Show us then,' Uncle Alun says.

Ronnie takes his hand and Florence grabs Aunty Gwen's. They follow me through the gate to the mouth of the hollow.

Uncle Alun pulls his spade out of the sack.

'We're going to bury him,' Aunty Gwen says, so quietly I can barely hear her.

Uncle Alun reaches in again. 'Here, boy.' It's the candlewick bedspread. 'It was Nye's before it was yours. I need you to put the – *wrap him* in it while I dig.'

He goes around to the other side of the tree. Mrs Thomas asks Ronnie to show her where the yellow flowers grow. It's just Florence and me left, and I know this is right. This is what we have to do.

The small space doesn't bother me at all. I pass each bone slowly back to Florence, counting as I do. She counts too, under her breath, as she lays them on the bedspread.

‘Two hundred and six,’ I whisper, passing the last one to her. They’re all there.

‘Two hundred and six,’ she whispers back.

I shuffle backwards and stand. Florence hands me the bundle. Neither of us says a word. We walk round to the patch of fresh earth behind the wych elm. Aunty Gwen and Ronnie come up to join us.

I offer him the bedspread but Uncle Alun shakes his head. I carefully lower it into the ground. Then we all stare down into the hole. Nye’s new resting place.

The Thomases are holding each other so tight it’s like they’re one person. Ronnie splutters and hides his face in Florence’s side.

‘It’s all right,’ she whispers, putting her arm around him. ‘We’re making Nye safe. That’s all.’

I try not to look at Uncle Alun because I know tears are running down his cheeks. Then we each take some earth and scatter it.

Florence looks up. ‘Should we say some words? Like in a proper funeral?’

Aunty Gwen looks at Uncle Alun, who just nods,

his face straining against whatever feelings are rushing around inside him.

Florence lowers her head. 'Nye, I'm sorry you died. We'll come here and put flowers all the time. You'll never really be on your own again.'

Uncle Alun lets out a strangled sort of noise. Ronnie shuffles his feet.

I put my arm around him. 'You don't have to say anything. Being here is enough.'

He leans into me.

Then it's my turn. I clear my throat, my heart pounding like a hammer. But it's like the words were already there, waiting to be spoken. 'Nye, I wish I could have known you because, if you're like your brother, you would have made a good grown-up. I don't know where you are now. Uncle Alun thinks nothing happens after we die but, even if that's true, it doesn't really matter because when you were here you were loved.'

I look at Uncle Alun, right into those coal-black eyes, and he nods his head.

I take a big breath but it doesn't stop the tears

coming. I try to wipe them away before Florence sees, but she just takes my hand and we all stand here together.

No one speaks. Even Ronnie knows to keep quiet now.

After a few minutes, Uncle Alun picks up the spade. 'This is my job,' he says, and the rest of us move away. We sit a little bit further down the mountain, Ronnie curled up on Aunty Gwen's lap.

But before Uncle Alun starts to fill in the grave he reaches into his pocket and pulls out something so small I can hardly see it from here. He kneels and puts it in the ground and I know it's the toy soldier. He covers the bones and the bedspread and the drummer with earth, then stands, leaning on his spade, his head down.

Aunty Gwen moves Ronnie off her lap and goes to her husband. She crouches and lays the yellow flowers down.

'Those need water,' Florence says to me. 'I'll bring a jam jar tomorrow.'

Aunty Gwen lets out a sob; Uncle Alun helps her to her feet and pulls her close to him.

I tap Ronnie on the shoulder and give Florence a nod. 'Let's go.'

Aunty Gwen and Uncle Alun stay under the tree for ages. Florence and me sit on a big tree stump at the bottom of the field. Ronnie's on the grass in front of us.

'I want to pick some flowers for Aunty Gwen to keep,' he says.

Florence stands. 'That's a nice idea. Coming, Jimmy?'

I shake my head.

Aunty Gwen and Uncle Alun walk down the field. She kisses his cheek, then goes to join Ronnie and Florence, a small smile on her face. They rush to her, hold hands in a circle and spin around. Ronnie loves ring-a-ring o' roses. He likes being a cow in the meadow.

I move for Uncle Alun to sit on the tree stump with me. 'Don't fancy playing then, Jimmy?'

I shrug. 'Not really.'

'You *can* enjoy yourself, you know, here I mean, in Llanbryn. You don't always have to fight against it.' He touches his ribs and winces.

'Are you all right?'

He looks at me, just like he did that first time in the living room when I saw his eyes were like coal. I think a bit of the shine's come back to them.

'I will be, boy. Thanks to you.'

'*Me?*'

'Yes.' He lowers his head for a second, then squints into the afternoon sun. 'You found my brother.' He twists his wedding ring and sighs. 'Your Aunty Gwen wasn't sure about this. You know she's chapel, and that means she holds store by tradition and God.'

'Not that much though – she married you.'

He smiles a small smile. 'True. She thought Nye should have a proper funeral, a coffin, prayers from a minister, that sort of thing. But I said he stays where he is. He's my brother. By her reckoning – and I'm not saying she's right, mind you – this is all God's land,

and Nye's staying put. You found him and kept him safe. That's good enough for me.'

I feel his large, strong hand on my shoulder.

'It's done,' he says.

CHAPTER THIRTY-EIGHT

THREE IN A ROW

'He's gone?' I ask, chasing a blackberry around my bowl with a spoon. 'Not just for a visit? Properly gone?'

'That's what Phyllis said.' Aunty Gwen pours the last of the evaporated milk on to Uncle Alun's pie. He winks at her. 'Duff *and* his sister, straight back to London. They were a bad influence on Jack, apparently.' She rolls her eyes.

'After what he did to Ronnie,' Florence says, clanking her spoon against the side of her bowl, 'it'd serve him right if a bomb landed on him.'

'Now now, Flossie,' Uncle Alun says. 'Even a horror like him doesn't deserve that.'

Florence's cheeks go a bit pink.

So Duff's been sent back home. Good.

'Will they be evacuated again?' Ronnie asks.

'Probably,' Aunty Gwen says, 'and perhaps he will have learned his lesson.'

'I should think he has,' Uncle Alun says. 'Don't mess with Flossie and the boys.'

Florence, Ronnie and me laugh. It's nice to have her here for dinner.

'Well, that wasn't quite what I meant.' Aunty Gwen can't help but smile though.

'Maybe he learned not to be such a stupid pig-face?' suggests Ronnie.

Florence howls with laughter and we all join in, even Aunty Gwen.

Uncle Alun's ribs aren't as sore now. Aunty Gwen says she can tell he's on the mend because he's complaining the doctors won't let him do any digging. I can't believe it's been a week since they pulled him out of the pit.

Ronnie's finished before everyone else and is quietly driving his Dinky van up and down my leg. It tickles and I squirm.

'What's up with you?' Florence asks.

'He's got ants in his pants!' Ronnie squeals.

Aunty Gwen frowns, lifting the cloth and leaning down. 'Ronnie Travers, how many times have I told you not to bring that van to the table?'

He looks like he's working that out, then he tries his best doe eyes. 'I thought it wasn't allowed *on* the table.'

'Is that so?'

'Ahh, leave him, Gwen,' Uncle Alun says. 'He's doing no harm.'

He holds out his hand and my little brother drives the van along it.

'Do this,' Ronnie says, showing his palm. Uncle Alun copies. Ronnie puts his own little hand underneath Uncle Alun's and squeezes it so it makes a dip, then he drives his van up the hairy arm. 'Now I'm driving *through the valley and up the mountains*.'

He says it with such a Welsh accent that we all laugh.

Uncle Alun watches the yellow van. 'It's good for a little fella to have a toy he loves,' he says quietly. He looks at Aunty Gwen and she nods. He gets up and leaves the kitchen.

'Where's he gone?' Ronnie asks.

Aunty Gwen shakes her head and smiles. 'You'll see.'

When he comes back, Uncle Alun is holding a flat red box. He sits down, lays it on the table and lifts the lid. Inside, a label says *Types of the British Army no. 102*.

'Soldiers!' Ronnie cries.

'You can play with them for as long as you're here … and maybe after the war too.' He glances at Aunty Gwen, whose eyes are shining with tears. 'If you'd like to come and visit us.'

I can't stop myself. I push back my chair, leap up, and wrap my arms around him. He puts a hand over one of mine and squeezes.

Ronnie pokes a finger in the empty space in the cardboard box where the drummer used to be.

Uncle Alun watches. 'I know there's one missing, but …'

'It's not missing,' I say. 'We know where it is.'

Aunty Gwen let us off the washing-up because we've helped so much in the garden this past week. Florence, Ronnie and me are almost at the end of Heol Mabon when we hear voices from around the corner – and the sharp clip-clop of shoes.

'Jack and his father!' I grab Ronnie and Florence, and we stop to listen.

'What's the matter *now*?' says Reverend Evans.

'Nothing, I'm just tying my shoelace.'

'Well, hurry up about it. Mrs Maddock will be waiting.'

Mrs Maddock? Nosy old tortoise-next-door Mrs Maddock?

'But Dad,' Jack whines. 'I don't want to read the scriptures to her. She's ancient and her house smells like sprouts.'

He has to sit with her and read the Bible! Fantastic!

'Don't question my judgement, boy. And I'm taking you right to the door. You're not sneaking off with those oafs like last time.'

'I didn't—'

'Don't lie to me. Mrs Maddock told me you didn't turn up.'

The clip-clop of the vicar's shoes starts again. Any second now they'll see us. Ronnie's got a fierce look on his face. He's got some guts, my little brother.

'I didn't sneak off with the twins.' Jack sounds more cross than whiny now. 'They aren't allowed to play with me any more.'

'Good! Keep you away from temptation. Just look at how that Duffy boy corrupted you! Too easily led, you are, you need to grow a backbone.'

Easily led? Reverend Evans is easily fooled, more like.

'Shamed me, you have, Jack. Shamed me to the core. *Thou shalt not steal*, and what do you do? Pilfer like a street urchin!'

They both stop with a jolt when they come round the corner. Florence, Ronnie and me spread out, blocking the pavement. It isn't planned; it's instinct.

I shove my hands deep into my pockets and look Jack's dad square in the eye. 'Afternoon, Rev.'

His lips move but no words come out. I think he might explode.

'What's that you're trying to say?' Florence stares right at him. 'Could it be an apology for accusing us of stealing the collection money?'

Reverend Evans's eyes bulge, and he splutters, a bit of spit coming out of his mouth.

'Yuck!' Ronnie says to Jack. 'Your dad just dribbled.'

The vicar pushes past us, grabbing Jack by the collar and dragging him up the street.

'No?' Florence calls after them. 'Maybe tomorrow? I'll be in the shop.'

Ronnie and me laugh. Phyllis has banned Jack's family from D. Hughes Ltd.

'Florence, you're *brilliant*!' Ronnie wraps his arms around her waist and she cuddles him. 'Isn't she, Jimmy?'

'She is,' I say. Ronnie opens his arms, inviting me to join in. I step back. 'Get lost, she's not that brilliant.'

I lead the way across the Bryn, over the fence and up the sloping field, my legs not aching at all.

We sit on the gate with the tree at our backs, three in a row with Ronnie in the middle. Patches of the mountain are turning brown and red. Autumn is definitely here. I pull my coat around me. 'We had a letter from our dad this morning.'

'Did you?' Florence says. 'What did he write?'

'The usual – how he's missing us, Nan's making us up a parcel, no bombs on Islington yet.'

'Do you miss him too?'

I think for a minute. 'Yeah, but it's getting easier.' I hadn't realised that until now. 'He said he hopes we aren't finding the countryside dull.'

'Well …' She giggles, scrunching up her face. 'Nothing much has happened so far.'

We grin at each other over Ronnie's head.

Florence looks out towards the coal tips. 'No one writes to me.' But she doesn't sound sad.

'I'll write you a letter, Florence,' Ronnie says. 'I can spell your name now, Uncle Alun's been teaching me.'

'Has he?' She beams.

'Yes, and it's properly Florence, not Flossie.'

'Only Alun calls me Flossie,' she says.

I point to a bare patch of earth further along the hedgerow. 'Why don't you show her, Ronnie? Use a stick to write her name.'

'Yes!' He jumps off the gate, stumbles, and falls on his backside. He makes a big show of rolling down the field before getting up and laughing. A lot of things have changed but not how daft my little brother is.

Florence gets down and takes his hand. They go in search of a good writing stick.

I stand and balance on the gate, looking at the tree, like the day I found the skull. Uncle Alun says we can plant some flowers, like on the top of the shelter. I turn and look out over Llanbryn. Coal tips and houses stuck on the side of a mountain might be a different type of countryside, but it's my type of countryside now. A deep whistle sounds through the valley and smoke puffs up in thick clouds. The train picks up speed, on its way out of Wales and into England.

Without me.

But that's all right.

THERE'S ONE MORE MYSTERY TO SOLVE ...

While reading this book, did you notice something different? Something unusual? Did you see that on some pages the numbers have been replaced by letters? You might even have been trying to work out why.

An extra clue has been hidden for you to find. But how do you solve it? If you'd rather work it out for yourself then READ NO FURTHER! Off you go and crack it! But if you'd like a little bit of help, read on ...

On page 171, Jimmy is in his bedroom, looking at a flip book. If you use this book in the same way, you'll find the extra clue. So – start at the back and flip through to the beginning, keeping your eyes on the left-hand pages, and all will be revealed. There are a lot of letters, so you might need a pencil and paper to jot them down as they turn into ... well ... that's for you to find out, and when you have – WELL DONE! You uncovered a clue that not even Jimmy, Florence or Ronnie discovered!

This one is just for you. I hope you enjoy working it out.

lesley

ACKNOWLEDGEMENTS

To the wonderful team at Bloomsbury Children's, especially my incredible editor Zöe Griffiths, for allowing me time to settle and grow, for helping to shape my story into the best it can be, and for always telling me I can do this.

Fliss Stevens for overseeing edits with such skill and patience. And to Beatrice Cross and Jade Westwood – a Publicity and Marketing dream team.

David Dean and Jet Purdie for interpreting my words so beautifully and creating illustrations, lettering and a cover I absolutely love.

Amber Caravéo, you are everything I hoped to find in an agent: the perfect mix of talent, kindness, tenacity and Duranie.

Julia Green and all the brilliant tutors and students of the MA in Writing for Young People at Bath Spa University. Particular thanks to my manuscript tutor Janine Amos, who loved Jimmy from the very start, and to Steve Voake for the little task which grew into this whole book. Special thanks to Becca Moses-Paterson and Kel Duckhouse for being my MA girls.

Emma Carroll and Perdita Cargill for the belief and huge laughs, and James Nicol for cake and chat and writing days.

Katherine Richards, Matt Farrell, Lesley and Alan Hoskins, Julie du Plessis, Maureen Neal, Tarnjit Tiyur, Tim Wagg, Christine Oscroft and the Hutchessons for believing in me before this all really began.

Abi Elphinstone, Julie Pike, Nicci Rodie and Kirsty Applebaum for wisdom and friendship – and also to Kirsty's parents, Alan and Janice Whittle, for the evacuee chat and the best quiche ever.

The Richardsons – Debbie, Robert, Charlotte, Tom and Louis – your love and support mean the world.

Cathryn Norris and Jo Clarke for always being there, and Lee Newbery for being lush (mun).

The Maltese Tenor, Joseph Calleja, for making

even the tricky writing days better with your beautiful voice.

All the lovely children I have taught, but especially those of Stonebroom, Silverhill and Tupton Primary Schools.

Deborah Girling, for everything.

Jon, I couldn't have done this without you. You're *my* Alun Thomas and I love you.

Q&A WITH THE AUTHOR

1. ***The Valley of Lost Secrets* is your first novel. Did you always want to be a writer? How did you begin?**

When I was a child, I was always writing stories and poems. As a teen, I had many pen pals, so I wrote lots of letters, some of which included stories about my favourite band, Duran Duran. I suppose it would be called fan fiction today. Then life took over and the writing got a bit lost. In 2011, I decided to return to it and threw myself into becoming an author. I went to creative-writing evening classes and, in 2015, studied for an MA in writing for children. I love learning new things, so it was a dream come true. It's taken a whole ten years (probably longer than some of you have been alive!) to have my first book published, but it's been worth every minute.

2. *The Valley of Lost Secrets* is set during the Second World War. Have you always been interested in that time? What do you find exciting about writing historical fiction?

Sometimes people talk about which era they'd visit if they had a time machine, and I'd go back to the Second World War. It's always been the period which fascinates me most. The months from September 1939 to May 1940 were known as the Phoney War, because not much really happened in terms of fighting. But, for families like Jimmy's, huge change occurred in the form of evacuation. I enjoyed reading real-life accounts from evacuees, and was lucky to be able to speak to someone who was evacuated to South Wales with his brother – just like Jimmy and Ronnie. I also love the little facts I found out along the way, like how they used to get rid of nits, and that sweets weren't rationed until 1942. That lasted until 1953 though. All those years with only a small supply of jelly babies – imagine that!

3. **You also set the story in Wales, where you grew up. How important was it to you to bring alive both that country and that kind of community for readers?**

   My own village, Cwmafan, is known locally as the Land of the Moving Curtains, which will give you some idea of how everyone knows everyone else – and their business! This might sound like a bad thing, but mostly it was lovely and friendly and, as I grew up, I knew I belonged. Yet for Jimmy, moving to Llanbryn is difficult and, even though he and Ronnie live with kind people, he feels very much an outsider. He experiences the two sides of valley life: the people who gossip and judge, and those who care and open their homes and their hearts to the children from London. This is a story where Jimmy learns that he belongs too.

4. **What kind of books do you like to read? Do you have any favourite authors?**

   I choose books to suit my mood and can leave a longed-for story on my shelf for ages, waiting for just the right moment to dive in. I'm patient like that – I never peeped at Christmas presents either! I read a lot of books for children and teenagers, and my particular favourite authors are David Almond, Patrick Ness and Emma Carroll. For laughs I enjoy Frank Cottrell-Boyce and Simon James Green.

5. What is your next book about?

Like *The Valley of Lost Secrets*, the story takes place in a small village, but this time the main character is a Welsh girl called Natty. It's set in 1920 when the world was still reeling from the impact of the First World War. And Natty has a mystery to solve …

6. What do you like to do when you're not writing?

I'm a big fan of rugby and can often be found shouting at the TV or watching from behind a stuffed toy dragon when there's a match on. I also love walking, cooking, seeing friends and, of course, reading.

ABOUT THE AUTHOR

Lesley grew up in South Wales and now lives in England with her husband and their rescue cat, Angharad. She shares her time between writing stories, teaching at a primary school and tutoring adults. Apart from books, rugby union is her favourite thing in the world, especially if Wales is winning. Lesley graduated with distinction from Bath Spa University's MA in Writing for Young People. *The Valley of Lost Secrets* is her first novel.

@WelshDragonParr